D0914546

THE LOVE
ASSIGNMENT

Other books by Tara Randel:

This Time Love
Melody of Love
Lasting Love
Hidden Hearts

THE LOVE ASSIGNMENT

•

Tara Randel

AVALON BOOKS

NEW YORK

Published by Thomas Bouregy & Co., Inc.
160 Madison Avenue, New York, NY 10016

Library of Congress Cataloging-in-Publication Data

Randel, Tara.
     The love assignment / Tara Randel.
        p. cm.
     ISBN 978-0-8034-9825-9 (hardcover : acid-free paper)
     1. Single women—Fiction. 2. Florida—Fiction. I. Title.

PS3618.A64L68 2007
813'.6—dc22

                                        2006101341

PRINTED IN THE UNITED STATES OF AMERICA
ON ACID-FREE PAPER
BY HADDON CRAFTSMEN, BLOOMSBURG, PENNSYLVANIA

To Boone Charoenset, for your unwavering support, enthusiasm, and most of all, for being a good friend.

Chapter One

*W*hat am I doing here?

Jenny Meyer blew out a deep breath and gazed around the nearly empty Clearwater Sports Grille. Kate told her this local hang-out filled up on Sunday night after local softball games. That explained the blaring television sets mounted in every corner of the building, waiting for the rowdy game players to arrive. But without many patrons present, someone must have canceled the game and forgot to tell her.

She couldn't wait to hear the hair-brained excuse her best friend would use to explain why she was running twenty minutes past the appointed meeting time. Just a few more minutes, then she'd leave.

Why on earth had she gone along with this half-baked scheme anyway? Right now Jenny could be in her office, drawing up the new proposal that came in today. She loved her interior design job located in Tampa, and really wanted to get started with her new ideas. She'd even brought along a notebook to jot down ideas, just in case she had time. And since Kate was late, she might get her wish.

When her friend first concocted this idea, Jenny knew better to than agree. Kate had a way of drawing unsuspecting victims into her unlimited number of schemes. Really, Jenny should be used to it by now. She'd known Kate since high school. They'd gotten into plenty of scrapes together, usually after one of Kate's big adventure ideas. Even the year Jenny was engaged, Kate managed to get them into more than one escapade than Jenny thought possible. She loved Kate, but her best friend had an endless source of energy. As usual, Kate had worn her down and now Jenny sat in a dimly lit room, alone, and suddenly unsure of herself.

The plan was simple. Hook up with Kate so she could introduce her to some of her male friends. Flirt for awhile, just to get a jump-start back into the dating game. Since the abrupt end of Jenny's engagement, she'd thrown herself into her work, and Kate didn't approve.

"How is it that you know a softball team full of available guys?" Jenny had asked.

"There's a lot about me you'd be surprised at." Kate winked, then grinned. "Besides, I want you to meet Mike. He has a friend," she ended in a singsong voice.

"I don't know," Jenny wavered. "That just doesn't seem my style."

"That's your problem, Jen," Kate stated bluntly. "For such a talented designer, you don't *have* a style. You just work, work—"

Jenny held up her hand. "Okay. I get the hint."

Not for anything in the world would she let Kate know how much that remark hurt. And just because it was true didn't make it less painful. Her past dealing with men, her ex-fiancé in particular, made her wary of getting out and 'mixing it up' again. She worked too many hours, and was happy to be by herself. Maybe to Kate that seemed boring, but she'd only been protecting herself.

John's sudden change of heart before the wedding really threw her. For her family and friends, she'd put up a strong front, but in the quiet of her apartment, she'd agonized over what went wrong. That lasted about four months, then she got angry. The anger lasted about three months, then she went numb. That lasted a few months more, until she felt relatively back to normal. A little battle scarred, but good to go. On to a new life. Jenny's love life was lacking, so Kate decided to help out in the romance department. Which explained why she was here.

Also, today marked the year anniversary of her canceled wedding. It seemed appropriate that she should make a major change on this particular date. At twenty-six, she knew she couldn't bury herself in her work any longer while life continued around her. That's probably why she sat on the tall, leather stool in the Sports Grille right now. To prove Kate wrong.

The door burst open and Jenny glanced in that direction. Two guys in muddy softball uniforms entered, exchanging accounts of the final play. They laughed loudly and joined a group near the back of the room. Jenny breathed a sigh of relief. She didn't know a thing about sports and would have made poor grades in the small talk department. But Kate would have handled them, just like everything else.

Jenny's gaze settled on one wall, decorated with sports memorabilia and old photographs. A vintage juke box, positioned under team pendants, blasted loud music. She rubbed her temples, feeling a headache coming on. Darting a quick glance around the room once more, she stopped when a dark haired man smiled at her. She nearly groaned out loud, hoping he was a figment of her imagination. With his spiked hair and Hawaiian shirt opened to the middle of his chest, all that was missing were rows of gold chains hanging from neck to navel. She frowned, turning her back to him as a clear signal. Stay away.

Grasping the glass before her, she took a sip of the cola and grimaced. Lukewarm. Another sign urging her to leave.

"Want a refill?" the ever attentive waiter asked.

She pushed the glass away. "No thanks. I'll be leaving shortly."

In an effort to appear cute, he tried wiggling an eyebrow, but it came across as a nervous tick. "I'll check on you soon."

Wonderful.

Jenny checked the time on her watch again and decided not to wait any longer. She grabbed her purse, crossed the wooden floor, and reached for the door, just as it swung in.

"Oomph!"

The sudden, sharp throb of pain pierced through Jenny's torso when the door made contact with her body. Her knees buckled and she reached out to steady herself. Her head made contact with a firm chest just as strong arms grabbed her, keeping her from falling. As the breath returned to her lungs and the shock wore off, she looked up into the concerned face of her near-assailant. Her eyes widened and she said the first thing that came to mind. "You're not Kate."

He smiled. "Afraid not."

She sagged a bit and his hands tightened, which helped, especially since she thought she might slide to the floor. How embarrassing would that be?

Looking up at him again, she hoped her eyes weren't as glazed as her mind apparently was.

"Sorry about that." The stranger placed his hand at the small of her back and led her to the nearest table, helping her take a seat. He tilted his head and regarded her quizzically. "Sure you're okay? Would you like some water?"

"I'm okay, but I'll take you up on that water."

Jenny watched as he strode across the room as though he owned it. His black hair, carelessly tousled by the wind, or his hand, fanned his collar. His serious gray eyes had been tinged with concern. He needed a shave, judging by the five o'clock shadow darkening his skin. His worn leather jacket and snug-fitting jeans had seen better days. Even his boots were scuffed. Handsome and scruffy at the same time. She liked it.

In record time, he returned with her drink. "I'm really sorry about knocking into you. Need anything else?"

"No, I'm fine."

"Okay. Look, I hate to leave you, but I have to met someone, so I'm gonna have to wait by the bar. Take care."

With those words he turned to walk away, giving a drink order to the waiter before taking a seat at the tall table at the opposite end of the room.

Jenny gaped. That's it? Take care? A gorgeous guy literally barges into her life and leaves her alone? She frowned.

Actually, she shouldn't be surprised. Guys like him, good-looking and self-assured, never gave her a second glance. It was better not to think things would change, she'd just wind up disappointed. Her ex had already proven that fact.

What about your decision to change? her inner voice taunted. She stole a glance in his direction. He took a long drink from his glass, staring straight ahead. Jenny found herself wondering what he was thinking. He seemed distracted, not out for a good time like the good old boys in this place. Maybe she should go over and flirt with him. After all, that's why she was here.

Her gaze traveled to the stranger again. He rubbed his hands over his eyes and rolled his shoulders. His body language screamed exhaustion. Physically or emotionally, she couldn't tell.

Decision made, she stopped the waiter when he passed by. "When that gentleman at that table over there asks for another drink, tell him it's on me."

The waiter placed his hand over his heart. "You sure, darlin'?"

"Just do it," she replied in her best no-nonsense tone. Then she sat back and waited. If she'd made a tactical error, Kate could bail her out when she arrived. She grinned. For the first time in a long time, she was actually enjoying herself.

Across the room, Nick Bryson tuned out the noise from the blaring televisions, trying not to think. He'd made the long drive from Palm Beach to Clearwater in record time. Before leaving for the weekend, he'd promised his construction foreman that he'd meet for drinks. Something about meeting his girlfriend's friend. After the major blow-out with his father, he wished he'd never agreed to be here.

Worn out from the tedious drive, he sighed and raked his fingers through his hair. The visit with his family left him bitter and disillusioned. Again. It was never easy seeing them. He made a point of keeping too busy to go home, but every once in a while, he received a summons. They weren't a close-knit family to say the least. A battle ensued whenever he spent any time with them. Everyone bickered, the atmosphere always thick with tension. Too many secrets. Too many lies.

His father had insisted that Nick come over. Nick thought maybe they'd play golf, maybe visit old friends. He should have known better. Charles Bryson has never approved of Nick's decision to become a builder. He wanted his only son to follow in the Bryson tradition. Banking.

Nick shuddered. Just the thought of working indoors for hours at a time made him cringe. He loved being outdoors, loved watching an idea he created go from paper to a designer home a family could move in to and enjoy. He was proud of his work. Nothing his father could say or do would change that. So an ongoing battle ensued. Nick frequently felt like the loser.

He took a drink of the cola, shaking off the depressing thoughts and hoping the caffeine would revive him.

Besides, he had more important problems. His construction firm was on the brink of going big-time. A local, very prestigious group of investors were looking into using Bryson, Inc. exclusively on Florida's west coast. His problem—the board of directors were very conservative. They wanted to make sure the firm they used had stable owners. Made sense, but the group also liked to brag about their family-friendly connections. Nick frowned in puzzlement. It was only a job. Why should that matter to them?

But obviously this was important, which put Nick in a spot. He didn't have a great relationship with his immediate family. He didn't have a steady girlfriend, didn't want a serious attachment, let alone marriage. He got the willies just thinking about it. So, no kids.

He'd vowed to never have a loveless marriage, so that threw the idea of wedded bliss right out the window. But he wanted, no needed, the contract.

He rubbed his gritty eyes, trying to wind down from the long trip. Suddenly a vague sensation prickled his neck, like a warning that someone was watching him. Turning a fraction, he caught a glimpse of the woman seated alone at another table. The same woman he barreled into earlier tonight. She'd been looking straight at him, then lowered her head to inspect her glass when he looked over. Great. Just what he needed.

He'd never liked women coming on to him, trying to buy his time with a drink or two. He'd spent many years enduring the society parties at home and he'd grown tired of the mating game. Now, weary and spent, he realized he'd have to create a diversion. He anticipated her move, but she just sat there. Obviously not an expert at the game.

He eyed her again. She was pretty enough, he supposed. A cool-blond, all business and no pleasure persona. Not his usual type. Still, he found himself stealing glances anyway.

Her shoulder-length hair swirled around her face and she had deep set eyes, although he couldn't make out the color in the dim lighting of the room. She wore a fitted white blouse with large gold buttons and a black skirt. Her legs were bare, ending in high-heeled sandals. I'll bet she's always color-coordinated, he thought. He polished off his cola, thinking that her legs looked pretty good, and signaled the waiter for another.

"This one's from the lady over there." The waiter nodded in her direction.

Maybe he'd read her wrong. Maybe it was just thanks for not leaving her unconscious when he banged her with the door. "Tell her thanks." He glanced in her direction, frowning at the expectant look on her face. Holding up the glass he nodded, but not before seeing her eyes widen in what he read as wounded disappointment. That look drew him as no other come-on could. Innocent and honest. Visibly hurt. Jeez. He'd managed to injure her twice since he'd arrived. And they hadn't even been formally introduced.

He hadn't expected this twinge of, what?—discomfort, in a long time. That, alone, intrigued him.

Embarrassed by her dumb move, Jenny lowered her gaze from the hunk across the room. Just a nod without a word? The waiter approached with a grin on his face. "The guy over there said thanks."

"That's all?"

"Yep, that's all."

Great. What made her do such a foolish thing? Of course! The bump on the head! In her burst of confidence, she actually assumed he would come and thank her in person. After all, isn't that what guys hoped for when they bought a girl a drink? Or, had she been out of the dating loop so long that the rules had changed? She sat there, amazed at feeling on top of the world one moment and miserable the next.

Cigarette smoke burned her eyes. The stuffy room grew warm as more of a crowd filed in and the sound of the chatter over the juke box increased by several decibels. People were laughing and having a good time. Everyone but her.

She glanced at her watch. Time to go home. Gathering her purse and change with the intention of leaving, she swung around to stand, but a man blocked her exit.

Taken aback, Jenny caught her breath. Mr. Good-looking stood right next to her, a smile tugging at his lips. He leaned against the tall table and she realized he was waiting for her response. Unfortunately, she didn't have one.

"You bought me a drink, so I decided to come over and thank you." He glanced down at her purse in hand. "Leaving?"

"I've been stood up. I decided not to prolong the agony any longer."

Humor glowed in his eyes. "Looks like we're in the same boat. The people I came to meet are no-shows."

A suspicion nagged at her. "Let me guess. Mike and Kate?"

He laughed. "The same. I'm Nick Bryson."

"Jenny Meyer."

"Sit down and tell me what you're doing in this place, Jenny Meyer. I take it you're not a regular?"

She sat down, drawing her purse tightly between her fingers. She lifted her chin. "Why would you think that?"

He nodded toward the exit. "This is the second time you've tried to run out the door."

With those words, she relaxed. "Kate talked me into coming here. It's just like her to set a date then blow me off."

"Nice friend," he murmured.

"She really is, just a bit forgetful at times. Besides, her heart was in the right place when she bullied me into coming here."

"Excuse me?"

"That sounded all wrong."

The waiter passed by and she asked for another cola. Seeing the confusion on Nick's face, she explained. If he knew Kate, he'd understand.

"I'm getting back into the dating game and Kate was going to help me brush-up on my social skills." The idea sounded even more hair-brained when she said it out loud.

Nick's eyebrows rose.

She panicked momentarily. Another blunder? Why was she telling him all this? She should forget the whole thing. Standing, she brushed against him, ready to leave. The humor in his voice stopped her.

"So what you're saying is, Kate wanted you to have dating lessons?"

She shrugged with a nonchalance she didn't feel. "You know, for when Mr. Right comes along."

"Is there such a person?" Skepticism hooded his eyes.

"I truly believe there is for everyone, but I haven't found mine yet. Kate finds her true love with every guy she dates, but I'm more cautious." She bit her lip, remembering that Kate's latest love interest was this guy's friend.

Nick rested his elbow on the table and regarded her with amusement. "So tell me, Jenny, why were you out of circulation?"

"That's a loaded question."

"I'll just ask Kate," he threatened.

"And she'd love to tell you all." She debated about telling him her sob story. He seemed genuinely interested. Or she hoped he was interested . . .

"I was engaged to 'Mr. Right' for a year before he left me at the altar. It took me a while before I wanted go out again. It was Kate's idea to meet here and I figured it was worth a shot." She stopped and smiled. "The one good thing is that I got to meet you."

"You would have anyway, once Mike and Kate arrived. If they arrive."

Jenny checked the time. "I wouldn't count on them making an appearance. Something must have come up and I'm sure I'll hear all about it tomorrow."

Nick glanced up at the television for long minutes, then back to her. "Tell you what. Even though tonight didn't turn out as planned, you still want to ease into the dating scene, right?"

"Yes," she replied, caution taking a front seat in her mind.

"How about I help you. Dating 101, Nick Bryson style."

"You're kidding!"

Nick laid his hand over his heart, displaying mock hurt. "You don't think I can do it?"

Stunned didn't begin to describe her reaction to his offer. "I'm sure you can, it's just that we're strangers really."

"So are most people when they first start dating."

Her eyes narrowed. "Why are you offering to help me do this?" she asked, not convinced this was a smart thing to do.

"Why not? You seem like a nice person, even if Kate is your friend. And Mike speaks highly of you." He graced her with a seductive smile that nudged her curiosity.

"You can get a reference about me from Mike, if that'll make you feel safer." At her dubious expression, he said, "Look, I'm not seeing anyone seriously and I've got the time."

Translated: I've got nothing better to do, why not spend it with you? Not exactly the response she'd been looking for.

On the other hand, what could it hurt? Who better to teach her the fine art of dating than a hot-blooded, and oh-so-handsome, American male? Okay, Mr. Generous. Give it your best shot.

Then again, she didn't want Nick to think she was desperate. Thinking up a reasonable explanation for the lessons, she said, "Well, there is this guy in the office next to mine I wouldn't mind trying my technique on. He's kind of cute." She paused, drawing out the tension when she glimpsed the expectant smile on his face. "Sure, Nick," she answered sweetly. "I accept your offer."

"Great. I'll pick you up Saturday, around noon. We'll have lunch."

"I'll be ready."

Chapter Two

By noon on Saturday, Jenny had worn herself out with her frantic morning. She woke at seven o'clock when she normally slept in, then stood in front of the closet for more than an hour trying to pick out the perfect outfit. She had no idea where Nick planned to take her. He hadn't called since the night they met. After jotting down her address and telephone number, she'd expected a call, but heard nothing. Wavering between disappointment that he may have forgotten her and relief that she may not have to participate in this silly charade after all, Jenny decided to paint her toe nails a fiery red.

When the phone rang at ten o'clock, she nearly fell off the kitchen chair, almost smearing her paint job. Positive it would be Nick crying off, she calmed down when she heard Kate's cheery voice.

"Jen, are you ready for this dream date?"

"Dream date? It's only lessons. I told you that."

"Yeah, but you know me, the eternal optimist."

"I've been ready for two hours," Jenny admitted.

Kate laughed. "Don't let him know. Guys love it when you spend a lot of time getting ready for them. It feeds right into their already inflated egos, and Nick is definitely all male. Take my advice and act cool about the whole thing."

"I wish I could, but I'm nervous."

"Don't be. Nick really is a nice guy. Mike trusts him. If he didn't, I'd tell you."

"That doesn't say much, since you *and* Mike stood me up the other night."

"I already apologized for that. Look, Mike tends to get a little possessive at times and you know how I feel about that. We usually hash out all his problems, then things are better."

"And are things better?"

"Yes. He's learning to trust me."

"Like I said, are things better?"

"Funny," Kate snorted. "You know I don't like to be tied down. But I really like Mike and I'm working on being a better girlfriend."

"Good for you. But I'm the one going out with Nick, a guy I hardly know."

"And you will have tons of fun. I predict it."

Jenny laughed. When they were younger, Kate started ed predicting events in their lives. Sometimes she was totally off base, but amazingly, she was accurate most of the time. It was a private joke between friends, but Kate's sure tone had her worried.

"I don't know," Jenny sighed. "This seemed like a good idea the other night, but now I'm not so sure."

"Hey, you'll do fine. I may tease you about not getting out much, but you're a special lady and Nick will see that. Now, go out there and kick some dating butt! Show the male species you know how to party."

Jenny laughed as she hung up the phone. Why had she agreed to this outlandish idea? Jenny, a party girl? Yeah, right.

True, she wanted to meet new and interesting people. She knew Nick wanted to help, but what guy puts himself out there as a coach. Didn't he have better things to do with his time? Besides, Jenny didn't want to get hurt again. Nick Bryson was a heart-breaker, it was written all over him. "Stop it," she chastised herself. "Lighten up and enjoy yourself. Maybe you'll break Nick's heart."

One could only hope.

When the doorbell rang at noon, Jenny hurried to the hall mirror for one last final inspection. She brushed her hair loosely over the shoulders of a white sleeveless stretch knit top with a deep V-neck, smoothed her black slacks, and inspected the sleek crimson sandals. Taking a deep breath, she opened the door.

All her fears slipped away when Nick flashed her an easy smile. He cleans up well, she thought, viewing his neat black jeans and white oxford shirt with the sleeves rolled back to his forearms.

His gaze swept her from head to toe and she felt herself grow warm under his gaze. "Ready to go?"

"As ready as I'll ever be," she murmured as she reached for her purse and red suede jacket.

Nick led her to a classic black nineteen sixty-five Stingray Corvette. The car shimmered in the bright sunlight, the dark tinted windows lent an air of mystery.

"Wow, this is some car."

Nick helped her into the passenger seat. "Thanks. I'm a car buff. I love the older ones."

Nick settled behind the steering wheel and smiled. "Okay, here's the plan. Lesson One: get to know your date. The first time out is usually awkward, so I want to show you that you can enjoy the date with out the first date nerves."

"Fair enough."

"I thought we'd go to Tarpon Springs and check out the sponge docks."

"I haven't been there in years." Of course, she reminded herself, she hadn't been much of anywhere lately. But that had been her decision. As her heart slowly healed, she'd needed the solitude. Now she wanted to be out and about. And spending the day with a gorgeous guy was at the top of her list of things to do.

"I figured spending the day taking in the sights would be a good way to ease into my lessons." He winked at her and smiled, amusement lighting his eyes. "I take my responsibilities seriously."

Jenny grimaced at the mention of the ridiculous lessons. Some tutor he was, rubbing her nose in the absurd plan. But she had to admit, she did feel giddy at his attention.

Nick turned onto the main road. "Hey, what happened to Kate the other night?"

"She and Mike had an argument and she forgot to call. Typical Kate move."

He chuckled. "Poor Mike. I don't think he knows what hit him."

Jenny watched the passing tropical landscape and smiled. He sure had Kate pegged correctly.

Leaning back into the soft leather, she stared up at the cloudless blue sky. After a few minutes, she opened the window, filling the car with the cold breeze and the scent of orange blossoms. For the first time today, she began to relax.

Once they grew closer to the river, a subtle change marked the surroundings. A Mediterranean flavor charmed the tourist area. The air grew thick with salt stemming from the Gulf nearby.

Nick found a parking place, and led her down main street. "It's amazing how the people keep their heritage so strong. If you listen to the shop owners, you can hear them speaking Greek. It's like the old country. Several generations live here, keeping the old traditions. A lot of families could learn from their example."

A frown wrinkled Nick's forehead and Jenny wondered why he would say that. Before she could question his attitude, he steered her into one of the many gift shops. Florida souvenirs and knick-knacks lined the shelves to overflowing. Towels and T-shirts hung from every conceivable place.

"This stuff is hokey." Nick rolled his eyes, then picked a shell made gaudy by sparkles and bows glued to it. "People really buy this stuff?"

Jenny took the shell from his hands. "You're right, this is dreadful, but where is your sense of fun? Of course people buy these trinkets. They buy the memories of the vacation, not the stuff itself."

While Jenny lingered over the merchandize, Nick disappeared. She found him waiting by the door, a secretive smile tugging at his lips. When they stepped onto the sidewalk, he took hold of her arm and turned her to face him.

"Here's a memory of today." He handed her a bag. "You know, the lessons."

Curious, Jenny opened it. Inside was the shell he'd only moments before viewed with a critical eye. Gently, she took the shell from the bag, holding it close to her heart.

She looked up into his gray eyes and whispered, "Thank you." How sweet of him to give her this gift. Was the gesture genuine or part of the lesson? She couldn't tell from the bland expression on his face, but the intensity of his returned stare made her wonder.

The magical spell shattered abruptly when a small boy ran into Jenny's legs, nearly toppling her. Nick's sure hands grabbed hold of her. His touch warmed her arms, sending tendrils of delight through her.

"You certainly have a knack for keeping me from sprawling on the ground," she teased, fighting back a shiver of pleasure.

His eyes grew dark and he refused to relinquish his hold. "Just consider it part of the service." Scalding chills brushed over her just by the heated look in his eyes.

"Lesson number one," he said in a husky tone. "Never let your quarry know that you're affected by gifts this early in the game. Pretend it happens all the time."

His words effectively threw cold water on the magical moment. She glared at him. "Maybe it does happen all the time."

A knowing grin pulled at his lips. "Come on, let's go this way."

To her secret pleasure, Nick held on to Jenny's arm as they strolled down the busy sidewalk. Even when the crowd thinned, he still kept a firm grasp on her. She wondered if Nick's hesitation to release her had anything to do with the attraction she sensed starting between them. Really, though, how could she not be attracted to this great guy? It was strange for her. She hadn't even felt this way when she first dated John. This was only their second time together and she swore there was a connection.

Or it was wishful thinking.

They continued to browse through shops and historical displays, but the conversation stayed to a minimum. They stopped before a modern building that housed the famous Pappas restaurant.

"Ready for a bite to eat?"

"I'd better before I waste away from sheer exhaustion."

Nick grinned at Jenny's less than subtle hint that she was hungry. She didn't have to worry about wasting away, her shapely body had just the right angles and curves to make any man happy. Including him. If he were serious about this dating thing.

He had to admit, her outfit surprised him. After their meeting the other night, he expected her to wear something less playful, more serious. She looked like she just stepped out of a trendy magazine photo. And by the way other guys were eyeing her, he wasn't alone in his appreciation.

They entered the cool foyer and Nick asked the hostess for a window seat. She led them to a table looking over the river and the many large fishing and pleasure boats docked below.

He handed Jenny a menu, his eyebrow rising at her expectant smile.

"So, Nick Bryson, come here often?" she asked in a flirty tone.

He rolled his eyes. "That's the oldest line in the book. If you want to wow a guy, maybe you should think up something a little more original."

She glared at him.

He chuckled.

She had a way of making him forget about his troubles and just enjoy her company. "Okay, I'll play along. No, I don't come here often. As an architect, I've always been intrigued by this modern building slapped in the middle of this quaint town."

"You're an architect?" Her face lit up with pleasure. "I'm an interior designer."

"Small world," he muttered, thinking about the contract he was trying to land.

"Do I know your firm?"

"Bryson, Inc., located in Clearwater."

She frowned, her finger tapping her cheek. "Didn't you restore the old theater downtown?"

He looked at her with surprise. "Yes, we did that job."

Resting her firmly clasped hands on the table, she leaned forward. "I've heard whispers that your firm is up and coming."

"I'm working on it." But unless his personal life improved, his reputation may mean nothing. "Where do you work?"

"Nelson Design Group in Tampa. I also do freelance work on the side. I've learned so much about the business working with the Nelson's. And I can't complain, I'm always busy."

"Too busy to date?" he teased.

Her face blushed an appealing shade of pink. "Touché."

The waitress took their order and Nick found himself wondering about her. Why she wasn't out dating? Why had her fiancé left her? Did she still love him? He'd had fun with her so far today and imagined the more time he spent with her, the more he'd grow to like her. What guy wouldn't?

If he wanted to know more about her, he'd just have to ask. He was here to help her, right? So get on with the job. As he opened his mouth to ask her a question, she beat him to it.

"So, have you ever been engaged?"

His neck and shoulders tensed. He'd almost come close once, too close. Thankfully things hadn't worked out. He wasn't the marrying type. Instead of telling Jenny all this, he said, "Why do you ask?"

"Well, you know my story, and you seem to have this dating thing down pretty good. I figured you must have experienced it all, except marriage that is." She stopped speaking and her eyes grew wide. "You aren't married, are you?"

His stomach clenched and he ground his teeth. "Not in this lifetime."

She sagged against the leather chair. "Thank goodness. I never thought to ask you that."

"Don't worry. You're safe with me." He took a sip from the water glass. "So, why did your engagement end?"

Jenny winced.

"I'm sorry," he apologized and found that he really meant it. Just because she picked the wrong topic with him wasn't an excuse to be mean. She didn't know anything about his family or past.

Staring out the immense window, she gazed at the

sparkling water below and sighed. Now he really felt bad for bringing up the subject. "Look if you'd rather not talk about it . . ." he paused, suddenly at a loss.

"He was really my parents' choice," she began, flat resignation in her voice as she turned her attention back to him. "My dad met him at work and decided John was perfect for his oldest daughter. Dad brought him home for dinner and over dessert we found that we had a lot in common. Before long we were engaged." She pursed her lips. "I waited almost a year for him to set a date. He wanted to move up in the law firm before deciding on a definite time. Once he did, we planned and shopped and two days before the wedding, he called me and canceled. Turns out he started dating the daughter of one of the partners. I suppose she was a better career move."

What an idiot that guy was. And what a jerk he was for making her relive that whole episode. "Sorry I brought it up. You must have been hurt." He reached for her hand and clasped it firmly. His thumb danced over the soft skin.

"Not hurt," she answered, "just foolish. My family got so caught up in the excitement. I guess I let it cloud my decision."

Nick tightened his grasp. "Did you love him?" As much as he hated to admit it, he wanted to know the answer.

"In retrospect, no."

Nick breathed a heavy sigh of relief. Why, he didn't

know. When Jenny stared back at him, a puzzled look on her face, he asked the first thing that came to mind. "So how do you feel about marriage now?"

She shrugged. "The same. I want to get married. But it'll have to be for love, nothing less."

The food arrived and Nick let go of her hand. Time to change the subject again, for his own good. "So who is this guy you're trying to impress?"

Jenny looked up, her eyes blank for a moment.

"You know, the guy we're here for today. The lessons."

Understanding cleared her expression. The guy she'd mentioned from work. "Oh, he's a marketing executive. And a nice guy."

Meaning he wasn't? Or was he just becoming overly sensitive? In the short time he'd spent with Jenny, he found himself untangling emotional knots he hadn't even known he'd tied. How did she do that?

"So, when you hit the big time, will you be needing any interior designers?" It took him a minute to realize she was batting her eyelashes and smiling a cheeky grin. She'd assumed the role of flirt extraordinaire, and he almost missed it. He chuckled. She was on the way to becoming a model student.

Nick held his glass up to salute. "Touché."

She laughed, a clear, carefree sound he found himself drawn into. Maybe the fact that she wasn't the type of woman he usually dated made her so appealing.

"Your family must be proud of you."

The innocent comment made him edgy again. "Why

would you say that?" He knew he spoke too harshly, but the ingrained reaction took control. "They don't have anything to do with my work."

Her fork stopped midair. "I'm sorry. I just thought you shared your success with them. Most people do."

"Not me. Not everyone needs the praise of their family or their interference."

Old habits died hard. His family wasn't even here and look how they managed to set him off. Now he knew he sounded like a jerk. He took a deep breath, self-guilt reaming him out as he looked into Jenny's hurt eyes. "I'm sorry, that was uncalled for. I get a little touchy at the mention of my near and dear."

Jenny tilted her head and regarded him with concern. He didn't want her to see his vulnerability. He could handle it on his own.

"It's okay," she assured him. "I used to let my family interfere, but not anymore. I still want them around when I need them, and I want them to be proud of me, too. I love them."

The waitress returned to clear their plates and Nick ordered coffee. "I'm not very close to my family," he admitted. "But that's no excuse for me to jump all over you for an innocent comment. You certainly couldn't know what a mess my family is. They are one topic I don't discuss with anyone."

"Maybe you should. You might feel better in the long run."

"I never felt they were worth talking about."

"I'm not an expert on your family, as you so bluntly

pointed out, but if you have problems, you should try to resolve them. For your own good."

The coffee arrived and Nick took a sip. The concern on Jenny's face was almost too much to handle. She crossed her arms over her chest, tilted her head and stared at him.

He chuckled, trying to lighten the strained mood he'd created. "Don't start with the psycho babble. I have no need for Dr. Phil."

She grinned.

Pushing the mug away, he asked, "So, how do you think your first lesson is going so far?"

She rested her elbows on the table. "Well enough. I must admit, I do feel comfortable being with you, bad temper and all."

His mood lightened and he grinned. "The object is for you to feel comfortable around other guys, too. Otherwise, there's no need for lessons."

"You're right," she replied, but he got a nagging sense that her thoughts were elsewhere.

By the time they finished the meal it was late afternoon. They walked back to the car in silence. Nick glanced at Jenny, wondering about her serious expression. She seemed preoccupied.

He really hated to do this, since he was a private guy himself, but couldn't help himself. "What are you thinking about?"

"Future lessons," came her vague response.

For some reason, those words made him nervous.

Chapter Three

"This is disgusting."

Nick grinned at Jenny over a bucket of wriggling worms. "No it's not. It's spontaneous and different, something you've never done before."

"That's true."

"Lesson two: finding out what your guy really likes to do and once you find out, can you adapt? You can never receive too much education on a man's favorite pastime."

"I hope when the time comes, he doesn't mind a concert or play, far away from any kind of bait." Jenny grimaced as she eyed the worms again. Sitting on a deserted dock overlooking a calm lake, shadows wavering over the water as dusk approached, definitely fell out of the realm of her usual activities. Just minutes before she'd watched as Nick commandeered two fishing poles, an assortment of hooks, sinkers and other fishing essentials from the house nearby and lured her to his favorite hangout.

She was at a loss. "I don't know one hook from another and I definitely do *not* want to bait a hook with those slimy things." She shivered. "I can't believe you went through all this trouble just to show me a good time."

He rummaged through the supplies. "Hey, I aim to please."

She laughed, sure he meant just that. "What if your friend comes home? Won't he be surprised that we're here?"

Nick shrugged. "That's what friends are for. Besides, he owes me, so I have an open invitation." He leaned toward her and flashed a conspiratorial grin. "Best of all, he's a chef, so I talked him into helping me out." He cupped his hand on the side of his mouth and confided in a stage whisper. "I can't cook."

If this was the worst flaw he had, she could live with it. "I'm impressed with your attempt at entertaining me, but it would have been more fun to see you struggling in the kitchen after the fish are caught and cleaned."

"More fun for you maybe. Besides, you'd change your tune when you had to stop for antacid on the way home."

She laughed again, finding that she did it often around Nick. The friendly banter relaxed her. Since they weren't really dating, no pressure spoiled their good time.

Which was good, since she'd dressed like he asked; a pink T-shirt, cut-offs and old sneakers. A definite departure from their last outing.

She peered up at the dark two-story house and realized that she'd rather have seen where Nick lived. To get an idea of what he was all about. But she found it extremely sweet that he went out of his way to think of a date more casual than being wined and dined in the traditional way. Which would be indoors. Without worms.

Leaning back against a wooden post, she watched Nick prepare the rods. Along with the fishing tackle, he'd also brought what he called—indispensable fishing stuff—which included a jug of sweet tea, two large plastic tumblers, chips and dip, strawberries and whipped cream, and a small boom-box tuned in to a baseball game.

"I thought sound scared the fish away."

"It's not very loud," he replied from a few feet away where he sat untangling fishing line. "Besides, this is a ball game, not some loud rock and roll."

"That may be so, but it's certain to keep the female fish away."

Nick flashed her a look of disbelief. Then his lips formed a perfect smile. Which caused her heart rate to double. He chuckled as he put the poles aside and poured tea into the tumblers.

Jenny took the glass from his outstretched hand. "I thought being here on a deserted dock would feel strange, but actually it's rather romantic."

"Now you're getting the hang of it." Nick lifted his glass in salute. "Here's to romance."

Jenny returned the gesture, reaching across the picnic basket to touch the rim to Nick's glass. A symphony of crickets serenaded them as Nick stared out over the water. The light lapping of the placid lake licked at the dock. An array of dark orange merged with purple and indigo, like a paintbrush stroke against the dusk sky.

Jenny's attention zeroed in completely on the man sitting so close to her. She inhaled his tangy cologne, let her gaze travel over the dark hair gleaming in the last fading rays of sun. Long fingers curled around the tumbler with unconscious grace, his lips curved in a relaxed smile.

She brought her own glass to her lips and grinned at his choice of attire. She loved the look, worn cut-offs, a baggy and equally worn sweatshirt with the sleeves torn off and paint splattered over the name of some university. His muscular arms bunched with no hint of strain when he carried equipment or readied the fishing gear. His long legs, stretched out before him and crossed at the ankles, had probably seen many a work-out. She couldn't detect an ounce of fat anywhere on his tanned body.

But for all his attractive physical traits, she found herself drawn to a subdued strength she sensed deep within him. A self-confidence. He knew what he wanted. And she was sure he'd get whatever he set his mind to.

"Finish your tea and join me." Nick stood and strode to the end of the dock.

Jenny took another sip, then rose and stretched. She'd grown content sitting there admiring Nick. A pastime she thoroughly enjoyed. Too bad he wasn't on the market. What good could come from day-dreaming over a man who seemed to want nothing to do with commitment?

When she reached the end of the dock, she sat down as instructed, her feet dangling over the dark water. Nick sat beside her, baited the hook and cast his line with a wide side sweep. The sun had just eased below the tree line, creating shadows over the water. She took the pole he handed her, then cast the line just as he had. It didn't fan out quite as wide as his, but once the hook settled in the water, her grip tightened at every small nudge.

"Isn't this relaxing?" he asked, patting her bare thigh in a brotherly fashion.

But his touch didn't feel familial to her. Her stomach clenched and her leg muscles tightened.

"Tell me, Jenny," he asked in a conversational tone. "Are you willing to walk on the beach at dawn? Dance the night away in secluded hideaway? Go for a swim on a beautiful starlit night?"

"Nick, you've got to be kidding. I'm the original stay-at-home-on-Saturday-night girl. The wildest thing I've ever done is attended my lingerie bridal shower, and I never got to wear any of it!"

"What a shame."

Heat crept up her neck and flamed over her cheeks. When her eyes met Nick's, she grew even warmer by the undisguised interest flickering there. She turned away to inspect her reel and flushed again when she heard Nick's chuckle.

"Besides," she informed him. "I didn't date much before or after my engagement. It sounds like I've denied myself some very memorable moments."

Nick yanked on the line. "It's a good thing we met. Now we can work on livening up your Saturday nights. Once my lessons are finished, you'll be the toast of the town. Not only will you dazzle the guy at work, you'll turn a few heads along the way. How does that sound?"

She hesitated. How did that sound? Overwhelming. "I'm not sure about all that. Let's just take this slowly and see if it's successful."

"From what I can see, speedy decision making is not your strong point. When you spend too much time thinking about things, the adventure is gone. Look at your engagement. All that time wasted and nothing came of it."

"That's not my fault," she replied, miffed by his accusation. "Well, maybe a little. But in the long run it was better that I didn't marry him. He probably still would have had a fling with the boss's daughter, then we would have divorced and the whole ordeal would've been worse for me."

She stopped to take a breath. Righteous indignation required work. "Besides, you make it sound as if my life has no excitement at all. My personality is different that yours, Nick. The things I enjoy doing aren't as dar-ing as you apparently like, and since I don't plan on making any major lifestyle changes any time soon, we'll have to work around that."

Nick rested the pole over his thighs and clapped his hands. "What a tiger."

Jenny shook her head and stared out over the water. The beginning of a smile tickled her lips.

"Your attitude will make these lessons more of a challenge, that's for sure." He drained the last of his tea from the glass. "Sometimes change is good, on either side. Okay, you like the quieter side of life, so we'll compromise. No sky-diving or race-car type dates. In return, you can take me to, say, a poetry reading?"

"Do I hear the word 'boring' hidden in there?"

He chuckled. "No. I suppose I could stand to slow down some. I'm not getting any younger."

"Right. You're positively ancient."

"Hey, thirty-two is a good age to slow down and get serious."

"As the esteemed head of your firm, it certainly wouldn't hurt to be more respectable."

"Funny, that's what I've been hearing lately." Nick winked at her, then dug in the tackle box.

"Are you really as reckless as you sound?"

He shrugged. "Let's just say I like to have a good time, try new things. I guess that might seem risky."

She thought about his reaction to his family and wondered if they were the impetus behind his actions. "Doesn't anyone worry about you when you set out on these daredevil pursuits, which I might add, seem like a lot of hot air."

A dark frown crossed Nick's face. In the final setting rays of sunlight, she saw him tense and knew she'd treaded on shaky ground.

"I'm my own man. I don't burden anyone with my problems and if they don't like what I do, then I stay out of their way. I live for the moment."

It sounded as if he was trying to convince himself. "How very hedonistic. Does it come naturally, or do you come from an entire family of thrill seekers?"

"It isn't a trait we all carry, just a select few. I learned well." The now blue-black night covered them, casting his face in moody shadows. "It's not that bad. You make me sound like the Big Bad Wolf. Maybe you'd better run home, Red."

"I probably should, but I'm not going to. Is that daring enough for you?"

"Very."

Suddenly she felt a very persistent tug on her line and jumped up. "I think I got something. Should I pull it in?"

"Slow down. Do you feel it again?"

She waited, but nothing happened. "No, I guess the fish swam away."

"You'd better pull your line in anyway, your bait may have been stolen."

She did as he suggested, and sure enough, no worm.

Nick took pity on her and put fresh bait on the hook. "I thought you new millennium women weren't afraid to do anything, you being self-sufficient and all."

"That may be true, but I can't go as far as touching

those wiggly things." She grimaced. "I may be a modern woman, but I still trust you males to take the lead with worms."

Nick laughed out loud and the approval she saw in his eyes made her tingle all over. She cast her line again, then squirmed around on the hard deck until she was comfortable, all the while aware of Nick's direct gaze. She felt the tell-tale blush sweep over her face and feigned concentration on the line, waiting for a fish to nibble at her hook.

Nick started the conversation again. "Do you still trust men after your fiancé ended the engagement?"

Jenny thought about that for a moment. "I suppose I should be angry, which in turn would make me distrustful, but I'm not. I had plenty of time to get over it. I think John did me a favor. I realize now that I wasn't in love with him. I'm not sure what my exact reasons for getting engaged were, but he actually saved me from a miserable future when he backed out of the wedding. I won't let myself be short changed next time around. I'd rather have nothing than be satisfied with second best. Marriage is for the duration. So I guess my answer is no, I'm not distrustful and I would like to get married someday."

Nick leaned his shoulder against the dock post. "You're pretty forgiving. I don't think I'd react the same way."

"What, you've had no bad experiences with love?"

"Me?" He laughed, but Jenny noticed the humor was missing. "How could I instruct you in the art of dating if I were emotionally scarred? I've never stayed with a woman long enough to form a deep relationship. I don't mind having a grand time with a lady, but once it takes a serious turn, I'm out the door. A long-term romance is fine for some, but not for me."

Well, I guess she knew where he stood. Still, he seemed to protest just a tad too much. "You sound as though you're running scared from commitment. Maybe you don't want to take the time and effort required to make a true romance work. It has its rewards, you know."

"Can't say that I've seen too many of these *romances* work. I, for one, will gladly remain on the outside looking in. There hasn't been a woman yet who has changed my mind." As Nick set the fishing pole down to refill their glasses, Jenny wondered where his resentment stemmed from.

"Look, I'm here for you, to give you confidence to get out and date again. You want to snag that special guy and I'm helping you get prepared. I want you to enjoy yourself while you search for the right one."

Jenny ignored the warning signal in her mind and continued to prod him. "I can't believe you feel this way and still claim that you've never been hurt. I think you're hiding the truth."

She knew she hit the mark when Nick leaped up and reeled in the line. Once he had it all in place, he set the pole against the dock railing. "We aren't here to analyze my dating habits. You wanted lessons and I'm trying to oblige. Let's cut the interrogation and have some fun."

He gathered some lures and tossed them into the tackle box. Jenny watched his every move, noticing how he held himself straight and stiff. She didn't care what he said, he was covering up feelings he refused to discuss. Even though she was smart enough not to push him on the subject, her curiosity grew in leaps and bounds.

With a sigh, Jenny rose, reeling in her line. The bait had disappeared again. All this trouble and no fish to show for it. Just as well, she thought. She wouldn't enjoy cleaning the scaly things and Nick would have gotten perverse pleasure out of making her do the disgusting task by herself.

After Nick collected the poles, he watched Jenny load the food and jug into the basket. He hated lashing out at her, but she hit too close to home and it spooked him. How could she be so astute about his inner feelings when he never revealed them to her, or anyone? Was he that obvious? He tried not to be.

The night blanketed them in darkness, the scent of damp earth and the lake captured by the humid night. As they walked to the house, he felt her body heat as she practically glued herself to his back, afraid she'd trip in the dark. He slowed down, taking the opportunity to enjoy her proximity. He stopped at the side of the house, dropping his supplies to rinse his hands under the outside faucet. Once he finished, he led her into the porch around the back and flicked on the switch. Dim lighting reached into the corners without ruining the quiet ambiance.

He retrieved the basket from her and proceeded to unpack, his wet hands slowing the process.

"And you think you're not domestic," she teased.

Nick shook out his hands, then tried to grab the towel she had just taken from the basket. She sidled out of his way, waving it just out of reach. He lunged and caught her, wrapping his arms around her waist.

Her squirming halted when she gazed at his face. The playful banter disappeared, replaced with serious intent. Jenny's breath caught as Nick studied her lips.

He'd spent the past week wondering how she'd taste, how soft she'd feel. His gaze gradually moved to lock her stare with his. It seemed an eternity before he read her surrender, but still he didn't dare move.

How he wanted to kiss her. He imagined her lips would be sweeter than the berries he'd packed for the picnic. He held back a groan, not ready to admit to himself that he was drowning in her presence.

The pupil had the teacher mesmerized.

He drew back enough to graze her lower lip with his finger, then teased her by brushing a trail across her chin line to her ear. She closed her eyes and moaned when he traced her earlobe, prompting his rapidly beating heart to race faster.

The soft sound she made brought him to his senses. What was he thinking, wanting to kiss her when he was supposed to be her dating coach? No commitment. No ties. And here they were on his buddy's back porch of all places. *You're losing it, Bryson.*

He gripped her arms and gently held her at arm's length.

Jenny blinked, looked around her, them wrapped her arms over her chest. She lowered her eyes, but not before Nick glimpsed the confusion swimming there.

Nick turned to the table to pour a drink while Jenny bent down to retrieve the abandoned towel. She held it out to him. "I believe you wanted this."

"You should have given it to me in the first place," he said, winking at her. "But then, trying to get it away from you was much more interesting."

Even in the shadowy lighting, he saw the attractive blush cover her cheeks. "I think we'd better leave before this lesson gets out of hand. By the way, you deserve at least a B plus."

She planted her hands on her hips. "That's all?"

"I don't want you to get cocky. You might decide you don't need my help any longer."

"Would that bother you?"

He grinned at the challenge in her eyes. "Yeah. I think it would."

Chapter Four

"**S**o why haven't I heard from you lately?" Kate asked as Jenny slipped into the wrought iron chair across the glass top table from her best friend. Kate had called the office early that afternoon, complaining that she hadn't seen Jenny in a while. They decided to meet up after work at Le Cafe, a trendy outdoor restaurant near both their apartments, for a quick bite to eat, and time to catch up. The spring night carried a gentle breeze that cooled the air, making the temperature just right for dining outside.

"I've been swamped," Jenny explained as she grabbed the menu before her. "A new job came into the office and I'm overseeing most of the work. I've been out to the site of this gorgeous new model home, which you would love. You should go out there. Maybe your real estate firm can work something out with the builders. Anyway, we're going with a Tuscan sort of style. I'm excited."

"I'm sure you are." Kate rested her elbows on the table. "You know I love to hear about work, but I'm more interested in hearing about Nick. How are things going?"

How were things going? After the near kiss out by the lake, she wasn't too sure herself. So she answered cautiously. "Fine."

Kate frowned. "Not the answer I was looking for."

"He's a great guy. We have fun together."

"I hear a 'but' in that."

"Yes, you do. Look, I have a wonderful time with Nick, but he's made it perfectly clear that he has a commitment phobia. Which is fine, really. Knowing we won't get serious sort of takes the risk out of seeing him. I'm comfortable around him. I can be myself. I like being just friends."

"So I guess he hasn't kissed you yet?"

A waitress stopped by the table to take Jenny's drink order, just in time to keep her from answering that loaded question. Once she left, Kate was all questions again.

"Well?"

"No kissing."

"Ever?"

"Kate, I don't know. I'm taking this one date at a time."

Kate pursed her lips before speaking again. "Are you sure you know what you're doing? Being friends only?"

"It works for us right now."

"I've heard Nick is a real heartbreaker."

Jenny sighed. Kate may have heard that, but Nick had acted otherwise. "Since we're not serious, it's not a problem."

"Hmm." Kate took a sip of her tea. "So what did you two do the last time you went out? You never told me."

"We went fishing."

"Excuse me?"

Jenny grinned at the horror on Kate's face. "You heard me."

"Why on earth would he do that?"

"I don't know. Part of the dating lessons. Actually, it was romantic in a non-dating sort of way. The lake. The sunset. Smelly bait. A night to remember."

And it had been. She'd thought about nothing else since she'd last seen Nick.

This was bad. She was definitely having non-friends-only thoughts about him. She'd better cut it out for her own good.

Kate still seemed to be having a hard time wrapping her mind around the location of their date. "This doesn't make sense. Fishing? Nick seems like the dinner and dancing type."

"No. He's really down to earth. I enjoyed myself." She laughed out loud. "Tomorrow, we're going to the mall. Can you believe that? A guy who *wants* to go shopping? It's lesson number three."

Kate stared at her for a long time.

"What? I've got something on my head?" Jenny reached up to brush her fingers through her hair.

"No, just thinking."

"Please, you never hold back. Don't start now."

"You just seem really . . . relaxed. Happy. Not so uptight, like you have been for the past year."

Jenny flashed her a genuine smile. "Seeing Nick has been therapeutic. He's good medicine."

"Just be careful you don't overdose."

"Jenny, there's a guy staring at you."

She looked up from reading the back cover of a paperback novel, curious at the amused tone in Nick's voice. He had picked her up earlier in the day for their shopping trip, in the guise of lesson number three. Come along while I run a few errands, Nick had said. All in the pursuit of research.

Okay, she could play along. Ask questions like, what did the male species like to buy, what stores did they frequent? So far they'd stopped in two sporting goods stores, a video room, and now they stood outside a bookstore, perusing the bestseller stand.

"What are you talking about?" she asked.

Nick pointed across the mall. "Over there, by the music shop. You see, the guy watching you but cleverly trying to hide it."

Jenny laughed. "You're exaggerating."

"No, really. He's sneaking glances this way again."

Exasperated, Jenny peered at a man standing before a display of CDs. When he turned toward her, she gasped in recognition.

"You know him?"

"Yes."

"Well, who is he?"

"My ex-fiancé," she murmured.

"Really?"

Jenny watched Nick's teasing smile of moments before turn serious. His eyes glittered as the man they were discussing approached them and took her hand.

"Jenny, I thought that was you. How are you?"

"John. What a surprise." She deftly removed her hand from his grasp and slipped it in her pants pocket.

He nervously pushed his glasses over the bridge of his nose. "I've been thinking about you a lot lately. Been meaning to call you." His eyes darting suspiciously at Nick and back.

"Why? We don't have anything to talk about." She kept her tone cold, amazed that she could carry on a conversation with a man who had humiliated her, while the over-eager dating coach she was attracted to stood by and listened.

"I know it's been a long time," John apologized.

"About a year, to be exact," Nick pinpointed, his voice heavy with sarcasm.

John's eyes flickered to Nick. "Who is this guy?"

"This is Nick, a . . . friend of mine."

"How close a friend?"

"I don't think that's any of your business."

Nick smiled at Jenny, approval clear on his face. If she had any lingering doubts, having Nick here proved once and for all that any feelings for her ex were dead and buried. Just when she started to breath easy, thinking that this brief encounter would be a breeze to handle, Nick knocked the wind out of her sails.

"Why don't we all go to the bistro at the mall entrance? We can sit down, have a drink, and John can fill us in on what he's been up to."

She didn't like Nick's terse smile. When she spoke, her voice rose in alarm. "I don't think that's a good idea."

"Sure it is." Nick gave John a friendly slap on the back. "What do you say?"

John looked at Jenny, a silent plea for help in his eyes. "I'd rather talk to Jenny alone."

"Sorry." Nick shrugged. "She's with me and I insist on keeping it that way." He looked around them then confided to John. "You aren't the first guy to hit on her today."

Jenny's mouth fell open at his bald-faced lie. What was he up to?

Before she could question him, Nick herded them in the direction of the restaurant. A chill swept over her and she wished she had a jacket to drape over the pale pink tank top she'd thrown on over denim capri's and low sandals.

After they ordered their beverages, Jenny took the time to study her ex-fiancé. He hadn't changed much, still sporting the preppie look; blond hair styled short, a light tan, from playing golf, most likely. The trendy wire rim glasses were new. There were lines bracketing his blue eyes and mouth, telltale signs that the law practice was taking its toll.

"So, what have you been doing?" Jenny asked with the morbid curiosity of a passerby at an accident scene who didn't want to look, but is curious just the same.

"Working hard at the firm. They've given me some high profile cases, plus a majority of new clients. I didn't realize how time consuming it would really be."

"Why not? You worked long hours when we were engaged. Or was that just an excuse for when you tackled other pursuits?"

John squirmed on the stool, running his hands over sharply creased slacks. "It's more work than I anticipated."

"Kills the dating life, doesn't it?" Nick remarked.

"Yeah," John agreed, looking glum.

Very subtly, Nick seemed to be testing the waters, fishing for John's real motivation in his renewed interest in Jenny. Did she want to know the truth? No, it was too late with John, she had no interest in him. But Nick seemed anxious to know and she had to wonder why.

She shot Nick a look that pleaded with him not to make waves.

The drinks arrived and Nick raised his in a salute, then sauntered off to a video game, leaving Jenny to deal with John alone. She watched Nick walk away and swallowed a rush of pleasure. Regardless of the fact that John sat mere inches away, she couldn't drag her eyes away from Nick's broad shoulders, lean muscle moving beneath his polo shirt as he played the game. And the ways his faded jeans hugged his hips . . .

A buzzing sound, like someone talking, gradually

brought her attention back to John. "What did you say?"

"I asked you a question. Are you serious about that guy?"

"What does it matter? You and I are old news. I've moved on with my life and it doesn't include you."

John sat back, a frown marring his forehead, but properly chastised in Jenny's estimation. "I can see that." He hesitated, his gaze raking her body from head to toe. "You're more self-assured, more in control. And you look good, Jen. Real good."

At another time, Jenny would have relished such a compliment from him. Now it sounded hollow to her ears. Lately, only one man's praise sent her pulse racing.

"Do you want something from me?" she asked, definitely sure she didn't trust his intentions.

John pulled at his shirt collar. "What makes you say that?"

"I haven't seen you in over a year. Suddenly we bump into each other and you tell me you were thinking of calling me? Excuse me if I'm a bit suspicious."

John's eyes darted around the room then back to her. "Look, I know I left things badly between us. I could have handled it better, but I was under a lot of pressure. Maybe we could make a fresh start, try again?"

Bitterness surged through Jenny. She clicked the clasp to her purse open and closed. Open and closed. "What happened to you and the boss's daughter?"

A red flush crept over John's cheeks. "She broke it off. Said I was too busy and had no time for fun anymore."

"So you decided to see if good old Jenny would take you back? That I probably wasn't dating anyway, so why not give it a try? Sorry. I learned my lesson the first time, John. I won't go back there again."

John scowled, but remained silent. He took another sip of his drink, then started to speak. Nick returned at that precise moment, cutting him off.

"So, how's it going, you two? Catch up on old times?"

"Yes," Jenny replied, her voice unsteady. "And this conversation is over." She slid from the stool, grabbing her purse. "If you gentlemen will excuse me, I'm going to the ladies room."

She held her head high as she walked away, even though her legs were shaking. Once she entered the cool bathroom, she found a chair and sank into it.

Her heart beat rapidly, but this time with anger, not humiliation. She should have known John would want her back only because he'd been dumped, not because he missed her. How she hated being second best. Even Nick treated her with courtesy while being honest about not wanting a commitment. If he wanted to date another woman, he'd have the decency to inform her.

Not like deceitful John. What had she seen in him? A steady Friday night date? To make her parents happy by seeing their oldest daughter married? She shook her head. The only pleasure she'd gotten out of bumping into John was the news that he'd been dumped. Now he understood her hurt, her disappointment.

If she'd been alone, John would have assumed she

couldn't get a date. Thank heavens for Nick's impromptu shopping trip. Being with another man proved to John that she had moved on. Successfully, thank-you-very-much.

She glanced in the mirror before leaving to make sure her run-in with John hadn't left her visibly rattled. Nick sat alone when she returned.

"Where's John?"

"It seems he had more shopping to do. He said to tell you goodbye."

"For good, I hope." Jenny suspected there was more to the story when she glimpsed the mischievous glint in his eyes. "What did you say to him?"

"Me?" Nick eyebrows rose. "You think I said something to make him leave?"

She placed her hands on her hips. "Yes, I most certainly do. And another thing. Where did you get that crazy idea that we should all sit down and visit like long lost friends?"

He patted the chair next to him. "Come on. Sit down and finish your drink."

She took the seat next to his. "Well? Explain."

"When you told me the guy was your ex, all I really wanted to do was take him outside and show him a piece of the asphalt."

Enthralled, Jenny leaned her elbow on the table and tilted toward him. "You'd fight for my honor?"

Nick's hand circled his glass, moving it around in the wet ring. "No. I'm a politically correct kind of guy nowadays. I don't resort to violence."

"Oh."

"Disappointed?"

"A little."

He chuckled again. "It made me mad when he came slinking up to you like nothing happened. Maybe I used the wrong tactics, but I wanted to make him squirm. I'm sorry if it made you uncomfortable. I figured once he acted like a jerk, you'd tell him off. Was I wrong?"

He wasn't, but why did it matter so much to him? Should she ask? Instead she said, "Actually, you weren't. His girlfriend broke up with him, so suddenly I looked good again. I told him I didn't appreciate his change of heart."

Taking her hand in his, Nick stroked her palm with his thumb. Tremors of delight danced up her arm. "Don't ever let anyone make you feel second best, Jenny. Not even me." He hesitated a moment. "I know you said you're over him, but tonight didn't make you change your mind, did it?"

Jenny's heart beat faster. He had that nonchalant tone, but the look in his eye said he was very much interested in her answer. Again, she wondered why. They weren't serious, had a nice casual relationship that made them friends more than anything else. Yet the concerned look on his face said more than friends. Like her answer was terribly important to him. Unless she was reading more into his gentlemanly gesture than was really there.

She pretended to think about her answer, repayment for his interference with John. True, the situation had worked out fine, but she wanted him to squirm this time.

When a frown darkened his face, she gave in. "It's really over. One hundred percent. I told you it was, but tonight's chance meeting really confirmed the end . . . forever." She tilted her head. "I didn't feel a thing when I saw him, although at first I wished you weren't here."

His eyebrow's rose. "Why?"

"I was worried about how you would feel meeting the man I almost married."

"How I would feel?"

She shrugged. "This isn't the type of thing that happens on a normal date, even you have to admit it, Coach."

"You get an A as far as I'm concerned."

"Thanks."

They finished their drinks and headed to Jenny's apartment. She invited him in for coffee, sure he would turn her down. After the events earlier, she expected him to run from her as fast as he could. She was surprised and delighted when he agreed.

Sitting on the couch with mugs in hand, Jenny kicked off her sandals and curled up beside Nick. "What a night."

He draped his arm on the sofa behind her, but didn't pull the fake yawn as an excuse to slip his arm around her. Darn. Didn't he find her attractive?

"It's over. Don't worry about it anymore."

"I'm not," she answered truthfully, wishing his arm would drop a few inches and touch her. Even if they ended up being friends only, she could have used a hug right about now. "It felt good to clear the air. Thanks, Nick, for not blowing the whistle. John would have loved knowing the truth."

"If he had shown up out of the blue when I wasn't there, you would have handled him the same way."

"Think so?"

"Yeah, I do. So quit thanking me."

They sipped the Mocha Madness, her only purchase from their outing. Soft jazz music spilled from the stereo, setting the atmosphere for intimacy. Would she ever get this romance thing right? Here she was, all alone with a gorgeous man and she knew deep down that all they could ever be was friends. Maybe she should start looking for some other guy to date. After all, she had to put Nick's lessons to work sometime, right? She sighed at the thought.

"You sound pretty contented," Nick remarked, completely off the mark at guessing her mood. That was okay, she didn't really want to discuss her thoughts with him now.

Moments later, much to her surprise, his fingers toyed with the ends of her hair. "I want you to know that I've really enjoyed going out with you."

"You're a good teacher," she teased.

"It's not like that. I'm comfortable with you."

"Like a pair of old shoes?"

"Don't. I'm being serious." He placed his mug on the table, then did the same with hers. "I haven't felt this relaxed in a long time. It feels good."

Jenny's breath caught in her throat as Nick lowered his head to hers. It was as though he was picking up where they left off the night at the lake. Only this time he lightly brushed her lips. She closed her eyes, shutting out all her doubts and eagerly returning his kiss.

His strong hand at the back of her neck drew her closer to him. He tasted like chocolate and coffee. When the lack of oxygen started to make her dizzy, she breathed deeply, savoring his tangy cologne. His fingers lingered over the sensitive skin below her ear, then her cheek.

Just when she thought she'd totally lost herself to him, he broke the kiss.

She opened her eyes. "Is something wrong?"

He leaned back against the cushion, a troubled frown marring his forehead.

"Nick, what—?"

He held up his hand. "Don't say anything. I should apologize. Like I said, I enjoy being with you. I just don't want us to get in over our heads." He stood, combing unsteady hands through his thick hair.

Jenny stood on wobbly legs, at a loss for words.

"I think it would be wise if I leave now," he said, searching for his keys. "You had one guy act like a jerk toward you tonight, I don't want to do the same."

Jenny followed him to the foyer, retrieving his keys from the hall table and placing them in his outstretched hand. She winced at the contact of her fingers against his. The electricity between them sizzled, still powerfully alive. Surely he noticed it? Why was he running away?

He paused at the door, gently brushing her mussed hair behind her ear. "I have to be honest, Jenny. The thought of kissing you has been on my mind a lot lately."

Her stomach tightened. "That's a good thing, right?"

"I'm not sure. I didn't expect it to be a problem." He sighed and looked over her head. "I need to rethink these lessons. I'll call you later."

With a chaste kiss on her forehead, Nick left. Jenny slumped against the wall, her heart pounding with unfulfilled desire and unfortunately, fear that she wouldn't hear from him.

Chapter Five

The following Friday evening, Nick stood at Jenny's door, debating whether he should knock. He'd come right from work, not intending to head in her direction until he found himself on auto-pilot, driving to her section of town.

With a sigh, he tossed his jacket over his shoulder, his finger hooked into the collar, then loosened his tie. He hesitated for long minutes, then, as if acting entirely on its own, his free hand knocked against the metal door. Maybe if he was lucky, she wouldn't be home from work yet.

He'd tried not to think of her over the past week. Tried not to imagine her justified anger over his leaving with such a lame excuse. Problem was, her kisses tasted too good. And his thoughts moved from kissing to . . . thoughts he shouldn't have. Liberties he had no right expecting from her. But her lips were so soft . . .

He groaned. He was used to enjoying a woman's company with no strings attached. He knew Jenny wanted to be with him, so what was his problem? She had every reason to think he only wanted her body. Shoot, he'd sure acted that way.

But that wasn't the case. Sure, her body did make his pulse race, but he'd gotten to know her and, frankly, he liked her. They had the same interests in books and movies. They discussed many topics and she was well informed about them all.

Whatever he felt for her went beyond just the physical. He liked himself when he was with her. He didn't feel so cynical, like the world was out to get him. He relaxed.

Then panicked.

And did what he always did when confronted with a situation he didn't want to handle.

He left.

All week long his thoughts seemed to center on her. Just when he would clear his mind of her smiling face, fresh memories would invade his mind. The floral fragrance she wore haunted him, her voice, laughing with humor, echoed in his ears. Before he realized it, he stood before her door, feeling as nervous as a school boy calling on his first date. As much as he disliked those feelings, the need to be with Jenny outweighed the uncertainty.

He breathed a sigh of relief when no one answered and started to turn away when suddenly the door flew open. Jenny stood before him, her brow raised in surprise. He also noticed she was dressed to go out.

"Hi," he greeted her. "Free tonight?"

Her eyes grew wide. "You're kidding, right?"

He loosened his tie more as he choked out an excuse. "I'm sorry I didn't call. It's been a grueling week and, well . . . you don't want to hear that."

She leaned against the door frame, arms crossed over her chest. She wore a bright red sweater and he had to fight to keep from staring at her soft curves. Tight black pants smoothed over her legs. She had her hair pulled up into a wispy, messy kind of hairdo.

"I'm a jerk, go ahead and say it."

"I don't have to, you already did."

His shoulders sagged with relief and he could see the humor in her eyes. "Really, are you free?"

"Yes, as a matter of fact, I am free. I thought I'd check out a movie." Her gaze pierced his, waiting for his answer?

"Lesson number four: don't be so honest. You're supposed to pretend you're busy so I can grovel at your feet."

Her eyes, free from guilt, met his. "Sorry, I guess I still have a lot to learn. Does that mean I flunk?"

"No, but we need some serious studying. How about going down to the beach for dinner?"

She didn't answer but looked down at the floor as she considered her decision. Her sudden distraction caught him off guard, then made him nervous when she started to laugh. "By the way. I love your shoes. New style?"

Nick looked down. He grinned in relieved amusement at the sorry state of his footwear. Mud caked into the leather and the hem of his slacks were dusted with dry dirt. "Do you like them? It's easy to get a pair. Just go check out a property for a new house, but make sure you wait until after it rains. Guaranteed to work every time."

"I'll remember that," came her wry response. "Come on in. You can clean up and I'll grab my purse."

Before long they were in the Corvette, dashing over the drawbridge leading to the beach causeway. An orange glow from the setting sun illuminated the Gulf of Mexico. Soft swells of water sparkled in the last rays of light.

He pulled onto the main boulevard, easing off the gas pedal as bathing suit–clad pedestrians filled the sidewalks overloaded with tourist paraphernalia. "I'm really sorry I didn't call this week. After the way we left things the other night . . ."

She nodded. "I would have called you, but I didn't know what to say. I guess we're in the same boat on this one."

"At least I gave in to my impulse to stop by your place."

"It's your lucky night," came her saucy reply.

"Very good." He chuckled at her come back. "There's hope for you yet."

"I have a very good teacher."

Nick pulled into the public parking lot adjacent to The Rockaway Grill. A crowd waiting for tables milled around the deck, already enjoying the start of the weekend. A cool breeze teased the spring night, so unlike the sweltering summer heat soon to come.

After giving his name to the hostess, Nick led Jenny to a railing overlooking the white sandy beach. A group of teens played volleyball at the net set up courtesy of the restaurant, providing entertainment for those waiting for a table.

"This place is great." Jenny's face beamed with pleasure. The light breeze lifted wisps of her hair. He had to force himself not to give in to the desire to touch her. "How do you know about this place?"

Nick raised his voice over the reggae music the band started to play. He found the noise a good excuse to lean closer and speak into her ear. "I know the owner. When he bought this building it was in pretty bad shape. I gutted the interior for him, then rebuilt it to his specifications. The place was run down, which made the job tough, but the results are worth it. It looks good, if I do say so myself."

"Please, modesty doesn't become you."

He laughed, marveling at how easy it came around her. He'd been so caught up with his firm, getting ahead, and battling with his family, that he'd forgotten about the pleasures of life.

She smiled. "Proud of yourself?"

"Yeah, I guess I am. I know I tried to convince you

otherwise, but it feels good to share successes with someone." He lightly brushed her hand. "With you."

Her eyes got that dreamy look and before Nick could steal a quick kiss, the owner came over to personally guide them to their table on the outer deck, away from the loud music.

Nick introduced Jenny and asked about the business. As the proprietor spoke, Nick stared at Jenny's profile as she looked out over the beach. With her hair pulled away from her neck, delicate earrings dangling against her creamy skin, he couldn't take his eyes from the sight. He turned his attention back to the owner before he went into major meltdown.

He enjoyed dinner with Jenny. She kept the conversation light, almost as if she were afraid to mention the night at her apartment. He couldn't blame her, he didn't want to go there either. That meant seriously examining his feelings for her. He didn't know if he was ready.

After an hour of good food and conversation, Nick settled the check. He nodded toward the surf. "Why don't we take a walk?"

"I'd like that. I love strolling along the sand at night."

With shoes in hand, they set off in the direction of the looming hotels and multi-level condos lining the shore. Stars winked at them from the indigo sky. The tantalizing aroma of food from neighboring restaurants filled the air.

Even at night, avid beachcombers dotted the sand. Nick watched families playing together, something he never bothered to focus on before. Too bad he never planned on having a family, even if he could picture it with a woman like Jenny.

A tightness clamped his chest as he took her hand in a firm grasp and turned away from the domestic scene.

"So how is work?" she asked.

"Busy. The new clients have a meeting set up for next week, so I won't have a minute to breathe. Keep your fingers crossed."

She squeezed his hand. "You'll do fine."

A shout from somewhere behind them stopped Nick in his tracks, his entire body going tense.

"What's wrong?" Jenny asked, concern etching her face.

"That voice. It sounded like my father." He craned his neck to search, knowing the gesture was futile. His father hated this coast of Florida. That's why Nick lived here.

"Does you father live on the beach?"

"Not this one." At her puzzled look, he explained. "My family lives in Palm Beach."

Her lips formed an oh.

"Aren't you impressed?" he asked with disdain. "Fun in the sun for the rich and famous."

She tilted her head. "Should I be? I've never met anyone from there, but I've heard it's a beautiful place."

He shrugged. "It's okay."

"Did you grow up there?"

Nick led Jenny away from the water, motioning for her to sit on the cool sand. He choose a deserted spot, far enough away from the crowds to go unnoticed, but close enough to still hear the waves along the shore.

He stared into the darkness, debating the wisdom of dumping his troubles on Jenny. She was right about one thing, he needed to talk, needed to get his problems resolved. Old habits kept him from confiding. Until now.

"Do you remember when I told you I don't talk to anyone about my family?"

"Yes."

He hesitated until she took his hand and wrapped it in both of hers. "I don't want to tell you everything, maybe bits and pieces. It's the best I can do."

"Nick, I'd like that, but if you don't want to—"

"I want to." He exhaled before speaking again. "Yeah, I grew up in Palm Beach. My dad's family is involved in banking, my mother comes from Texas oil. I have two younger sisters, both married to rich guys.

"All my life my father stressed the importance of money. You can never have enough, you know. No need for family or friends. Just the almighty dollar and the need to acquire more.

"With my sisters it was simple. Marry well. My dad wanted me to take after him, but I always loved to draw and decided to become a builder."

"And he didn't like that?"

"He humored me, thinking I'd regain my senses after college. But while I was away at school, I decided I had to be my own man. When I came home, Dad started bugging me about working in the bank, so I took off. Came here to Clearwater. Worked from the bottom up to get where I am today. No handouts, nothing from my family." A bittersweet smile settled over his lips. "My success really bothered my father at first. Now he's resigned to my future."

"But you still see them, it doesn't sound as if you've let go completely."

He shook his head. "That's true. I go back whenever they insist I make an appearance."

"They're your family."

"Yeah and each time I hope things will change and we'll be a real family. It never happens." Nick glanced at her, cringing at the compassion in her eyes. Who said confession was good for the soul? It only made him more resentful of what he never had.

"There are some other problems, things we don't talk about." He tried to pull his hand from hers, but she wouldn't let go. "I really had no right to criticize you about the relationship you have with your family. At least they care about you."

She reached up to caress his cheek. "You were lashing out at something you feel powerless over. My family is close, yours isn't. There's no point in arguing the differences."

Nick caught his breath, struggling to keep his mind on the conversation as her soft fingers traced a pattern on his skin. "How many in your family?"

"Two younger sisters, just like you. Mom and Dad are trying to get them married off. That's why I moved out of the house after the canceled wedding. I knew they'd get around to me again. They mean well, but I don't want to be part of their marriage plans. Once was enough."

Nick chuckled for a moment. "So you broke the family ties?"

"No, not really. I simply moved out of their house. This way I'm not smothered by their endless matchmaking attempts. I still check in, still get the fifth degree and lecture about being single, but its part of being a family. I love them. That will never change."

He thought about her words, then grinned and shook his head ruefully. "Some teacher I am. Dating is supposed to be fun and here I am getting serious on you."

"It's okay. I enjoy talking to you."

So do I, he realized. More than I want to. "No, it's not okay. We came here to have a good time, so let's get at it."

Abruptly he stood, reaching out for her hand. He yanked her up, jerking quick enough for her to lose balance. Just as he'd intended, she fell against him as she tried to steady herself. He wrapped his arms around her waist and hugged her close.

She looked up at him, a knowing twinkle in her eyes. "Smooth."

"Am I that obvious?"

"Definitely."

He lowered his head and nibbled at her lips. "You're too nice."

He groaned at the saucy smile on her lips, the close

proximity of her body. He liked her just the way she was, a bit naive at times, but desirable all the time. It occurred to him that if they weren't standing on a public beach, he'd be kissing her senseless. Where had all his trusted self-control gone to? Right out the window when he agreed to these lessons. For once, he didn't question why. He wanted to be with Jenny, no matter where or why.

"Hello? Earth to Nick."

Jenny's voice brought him to the present. "You looked a million miles away."

"But I'm back now." He stepped back, taking her hand. "Let's go. This hotel has a live band in the club. Let's say we dance the night away."

She cringed. "I don't know. My infrequent attempts at club dancing were a real disaster. Your feet may not appreciate my technique."

He tugged her along. "Not to worry. I can teach you a few moves guaranteed to outdo Fred and Ginger."

"It figures," she muttered loud enough for him to hear. "Is there anything you can't do?"

Yeah, he thought. Commit.

They entered the ceramic tiled lobby. He helped brush the sand from her feet, tickling her in the process. She nearly beaned him with her sandal until he left her alone, all the while loving her attention.

The bass-thumping beat lured them to the dance floor. Noisy conversation and shouts of laughter carried over the music. Nick held Jenny close, not willing to lose her in the crowd. He stopped in the center and twirled her into his arms before the people pressed in around them. Her serious expression as she diligently followed his moves made him chuckle.

"Let loose," he yelled over the music. "Enjoy yourself."

She shot him a dubious look, then shook her arms and shoulders, took a deep breath, and tried it on her own.

Before long, he lost track of the time. When the tempo slowed, he embraced her and rested his cheek on her silky hair. The floral perfume mixed with the musky scent of her damp skin washed over him. He felt her sigh as she wrapped her arms around his neck. The swaying movements brought their bodies close and since Jenny obviously didn't mind, he wasn't going to complain.

The music faded, signaling the band's break. He cupped her face and stared down at her, ready to kiss her, when a voice behind him purred, "Nick. Imagine running into you here."

Chapter Six

Jenny blinked and slowly pushed away from Nick. Tension radiated from him in waves as he turned to address the voice.

"Hello, Margaret."

"I didn't think you went for these spots, Nick. At least you didn't at home. Oh, by the way, I'm with Louisa. She'll be surprised to see you."

His tone went flat. "I'm sure she will."

Unable to stand the suspense any longer, Jenny stepped around Nick to face Margaret. The woman, much older than Nick, probably in her late fifties, stood beside them, a wicked smile slashed across her face. Her artfully arranged hair, pounds of makeup, and drop-dead gorgeous designer dress screamed money.

By the caustic tone of Nick's response, Jenny realized he was not pleased to see her. At the mention of the Louisa woman, he froze and his eyes narrowed to angry slits. She had an uncontrollable urge to reach up and smooth the lines from his forehead, but wisely refrained from touching him.

Margaret laughed, her eyes glinting with malice. "Do come by before you leave." Slipping her hand through the arm of her distinguished-looking dance partner, they made their way across the crowded room.

Nick watched them retreat, his stormy gray eyes never leaving the couple until they reached their table. Once they took their seats, he grabbed Jenny's hand and pushed through the lingering dancers to reach the bar. He tersely ordered a drink and downed it in one swallow.

Jenny stood beside him, wondering what had caused Nick's turn-about. One minute he had her wrapped in his arms, the next he needed a drink. What did that woman mean to him?

Then it occurred to her that only one topic made him this crazy. His family. She'd urged him to open up about his problems and vowed to help him. If it meant being patient while he dealt with his inner demons, she'd do it. The more time she spent with him, the more she decided he was worth the wait. And it would undoubtedly be a wait.

Her initial anger faded when she glimpsed the rigid set of Nick's shoulders. She placed her hand on his arm, hiding her disappointment when he pulled away.

He leaned against the bar, rubbed his eyes and sighed. "I'm sorry."

"Nick, who was that woman?"

"A friend of the family," he answered without looking at her.

"That's it? No explanation?"

"What more can I tell you? Besides, nagging isn't part of dating."

Jenny's mouth opened with a scathing retort, but she stopped herself. For now he'd clammed up and questioning him would solve nothing. Exasperated, she turned on her heel and weaved through the crowd in search of the ladies room. She needed a few minutes to calm down.

She held the door to the rest room open for a group of laughing women as they emerged. Just as she entered, she heard Kate's stunned voice. "Jen? What are you doing here?"

"That seems to be the question of the night," she snapped, then sighed. "I'm sorry. You didn't deserve that."

Kate waved off her apology. "Are you here with the hunk?"

"The hunk? Oh, you mean Nick."

Her friend rambled on. "You must be, you'd never come here alone. But the major question is, why did you leave *him* alone? He'll be snatched up in minutes."

"Good for him."

"Hey, why are you so uptight? Is everything okay?"

Jenny reluctantly smiled at Kate's motor mouth. It was familiar, something normal to relate to after Nick's stormy mood change.

"It's hard to explain. I'm not even sure what's going on."

"Are you going to be all right? Should I sic some of my new, and might I say, large, muscular friends, on him?"

Jenny chuckled and held up her hand. "Once I cool down I'll be fine."

"You? Cool down? I haven't seen you this worked up in . . . wait, I've never seen you this mad. First, Nick gets you out to one of the best night spots, then gets you hot under the collar. I don't want to interfere, but I need details here!"

"You? Not interfere?" Jenny parroted her friend's expression.

They looked at each other and burst out laughing. Leave it to Kate to lighten the mood. For once, Jenny appreciated Kate's party girl persona. If not, she'd have ended up brooding in the bathroom, forgetting her anger and worrying about Nick.

As soon as Jenny left, Nick headed straight to Margaret's table. Another couple sat with Margaret and her date, an attractive older man and a very beautiful woman with dark hair and gentle gray eyes.

Margaret noticed Nick first. "Louisa, look who happens to be at the club tonight. Can you believe we've run in to Nick? Ashley comes here all the time, but she never mentioned seeing you. She'll be so disappointed she missed you tonight."

Nick grimaced. Ashley was a pest, just like her mother.

Louisa looked up at Nick, a smile of greeting spread over her elegant face. "Hello, Nick."

"Hello, Mother."

Louisa stood, taking his arm to lead him away from the curious men at the table. They walked to a large window overlooking the hotel pool.

"Nick, I know you're surprised to see me, but you could be a little more friendly," she pleaded in a soft drawl.

"Does Father know you're here?"

"With Margaret? Yes, he knows."

Nick clenched his teeth at her evasive answer. "Does he know you're out with that guy?"

"Nick, it's not what you think."

"Why would I think any differently?"

Louisa sighed, then stared out the window. "You know your father. He's busy with the business and is much happier if I'm not around to bother him." She looked back at him, a shadow of sadness around her eyes that Nick had never noticed before. He shifted and turned his gaze away.

"No, he doesn't know I'm with Bill, but it is innocent. Margaret had to come to the beach to check on her boutique and Ashley, so I came along to keep her company. She's acquainted with these gentlemen. And she is the one who accepted their invitation to dinner and dancing, not me."

"And after dancing?"

Her eyes narrowed. "I go back to my room, alone, even though it is none of your business."

"Do you really expect me to believe you?"

"Yes, I do, but you want to think the worst of me. When will you let it go?"

He drew in a deep breath, pushing back the pain before he found his voice to speak again. "Maybe when you prove that you've really changed."

He thought he saw tears in his mother's eyes, but convinced himself it was just the lighting. An uncomfortable twinge worked its way up his back and around his neck. After a few minutes of mutual silence, he nodded then turned to leave. But not before he glimpsed the brokenhearted expression on her face. This time there was no mistaking it.

Jenny and Kate were leaving the ladies room when Jenny spied Nick leaning against the opposite wall. His hands were shoved deep in his pockets as he warily watched couples moving to the music. She took a deep breath before stepping over to him.

"Nick?" She reached out to touch him, then changed her mind. The fortress he'd erected hadn't come down yet. She wasn't about to tread where she wasn't wanted, again.

He turned his head, looking first at her hand, then piercing her gaze with his. He pushed away from the wall. "Ready to go?"

"Yes."

Kate moved up along side her. "Hey, Nick. Remember me?"

"How could I forget you, Kate? I have to hear how crazy Mike is about you, even when you two fight."

She raised her eyebrows in glee. "Really? I'm making him nuts? I thought he was playing hard to get."

Nick held up his hand. "I don't know, and I don't want to get in the middle. But please, ease up on the guy. For my sake."

"Okay, if you promise to take it easy on Jenny. She's spoken so highly of you."

"Until tonight," Jenny muttered.

"Really?" To her chagrin, Nick regarded her with a cocky smile, then winked at Kate. "And to think, she doesn't know me that well yet."

"I'm sure she will," Kate said, taking a step closer to hook her hand through his arm. "But if things don't work out for you two, I'm always available." She playfully batted her eyelashes at Nick, flashing him a cheeky smile.

"I'm sure you are." Nick deftly removed her hand before slipping his arm around Jenny's waist. "We aren't in any hurry to give up just yet."

"Says who?" Jenny countered.

"She gotcha there, big guy."

"I plan to change her mind." Nick stared at Jenny and she felt her face heat up.

"Humph."

Kate laughed.

Jenny tried to wiggle out of Nick's embrace, but he refused to let go. So she gave in and sagged against him. "Two against one," she muttered.

"But we love you anyway, don't we Nick?"

This time Jenny laughed at Nick's sudden coughing spell. Leave it to Kate to defuse a potentially flammable situation.

"My work is done here," Kate brushed her hands together as if removing dust. "Back to the old grind." She took a few steps then whirled around, pointing her finger at Nick. "And don't you dare breathe a word of seeing me to Mike, got it?"

Nick nodded.

"*Ciao.*" With a wave, Kate disappeared into the crowd. Nick leaned down to whisper into Jenny's ear. His warm breath sent shivers across her neck. "Now that girl knows how to flirt."

She gritted her teeth and forcefully pulled out of Nick's grasp, heading for the main door. She'd made it outside before he caught up with her.

"What's wrong?"

Disbelief flooded her. She stopped, turned on her heel to face him and planted her hands on her hips. "What's wrong? I'll tell you what's wrong.

"This night started out nicely, then progressed to the kind of date you'd only wish on your worst enemy. I feel like I just took a walk in the Twilight Zone. I don't appreciate this treatment, Nick, even though I have a sneaking suspicion of what this is all about."

Nick didn't like her words, didn't want to think he

was that transparent. He hadn't planned on telling Jenny even a small bit about his life, and now it came back to bite him. She had no clue that his mother partied in the building they just left, yet because of their talk on the beach, the intuition she seemed to have about him sent her in the right direction. The direction he refused to think about or discuss.

He ran his hand through his hair as he watched her stomp away. God she was gorgeous when she told him off. And she was right. He'd made a mess of things.

"Jenny, wait up."

She kept walking, forcing him into a light jog to catch up. She reached the car before he did, standing stiffly by the passenger door.

"If it wasn't for the fact it would cost me a fortune, I'd call a taxi," she told him.

He unlocked the door. "No. I'll take you home."

After he had her safely inside, he leaned against the car staring into the night. How could he make this up to her?

She refused to acknowledge him when he climbed in the driver's side. He started the ignition, then headed down the boulevard. For long minutes an unbearable silence filled the car. When he stopped for a red light, he looked over at her. For a guy who hated to talk about himself, he knew he needed to explain.

"All my life I've felt like an outsider looking in. My folks have secrets they felt it was their obligation to quarrel over, then get indignant when us kids didn't understand. They never bothered to explain, so I quit trying to figure them out and left." He tried to read her, but the red light glowed over her closed expression.

"I've never let anyone in, Jenny. Until now."

Her eyes blinked rapidly and he prayed she wouldn't cry.

She shifted to face him. "Don't you realize that if you keep pushing people away, you'll never have friends? A family of your own? That may not seem important now, but years down the road you'll become a lonely, bitter old man." A grin tugged at her lips. "And trust me, no matter how desperate I am, I will *not* go out with you."

How did she do that? One minute seething, the next she joked. Although it was just one of her special qualities, the whole package captured him as no other woman had. Still, the idea of being a couple still bothered him. What if he turned out to be unfaithful like his mother? Could unfaithfulness be hereditary?

The signal light changed and he continued driving. "Jenny, don't be nice to me. I don't deserve it."

She turned to the window. "Okay, Nick. I won't be nice. Now take me home."

She gave him the silent treatment on the drive home and as much as he thought he didn't want it, he kept waiting for her to say something. Anything. Name calling. Psycho babble.

By the time he parked in her complex, his nerves were stretched to the limit. Again he wondered where that steel control of his had disappeared to.

While she opened the car door, he fumbled with the

keys and jumped out before she got too far away. She waited for him on the sidewalk.

"You know, these lessons were a silly idea to begin with. I've had a great time, but I don't want to make you uncomfortable. Seeing you in knots like this really bothers me, Nick." She looked down at the ground, then back to his face. "I know it's because of me and I don't like being the cause."

"Why would you think that?"

"Because you're so even tempered with everyone but me. Am I really nagging? Do I spoil your fun?"

He hated seeing the self-doubt in her eyes. "No, it's me. I flew off the handle. But believe me when I say that you remind me about the good things in life. I need that, Jenny." *I need you.*

She nodded, but didn't look convinced. If it took forever, he'd spend all the time in the world trying to prove otherwise.

"Look, it's late and I'm tired. I'll see you later."

He escorted her to the door, feeling awkward when she unlocked the door and stepped inside.

"Good night, Nick."

Then she was gone. He stood there for a long time, an odd sense of loneliness consuming him.

Chapter Seven

Saturday morning dawned brightly, despite Jenny's dark mood. The rich aroma of brewed coffee filtered through the apartment. After pouring a mug of the steaming liquid, she settled down to read the newspaper, determined not to dwell on the disaster of last night.

Thoroughly engrossed in an article, she jumped when the telephone rang. She glared at it, debating whether or not she should answer. It might be Nick, but then again it could be Kate, or her mother. The insistent ringing grated on her nerves, so she crossed the room and snatched up the handset. "Hello?"

"Let me guess, he's there right now and you're ticked off at having to answer the phone. I'll call back later."

"No! Kate, wait a minute," she yelled into the phone. "He isn't here. We can talk."

"He's not there? You must be crazy. Nick has got to be the most gorgeous guy I've seen in ages. I still can't believe I didn't snap him up when I had the chance."

"Nobody snaps up Nick Bryson."

"What's wrong? Instead of acting like you're excited about dating Nick, you sound down in the dumps."

"We aren't dating. Its lessons, remember?"

"Uh-oh. What's up?"

"Last night was a nightmare. So I'm rethinking this whole thing with Nick. As a friend and a dating coach."

"Wow."

"Yeah."

"I could swear he has a thing for you and you know me, I'm a good judge of men."

"There's no 'thing.' " As much as she thought she wanted a relationship with Nick, it clearly wasn't in the cards for them. He had too much baggage to make a relationship work. And she didn't want to be his sounding board, help him fix the things in his life that bothered him, then have him leave her. As much as she didn't want to admit it, she'd moved beyond friend. Gone into the zone from which her heart might not return. She couldn't have it broken again, so she refused to go there. For her own self-preservation.

"Jen, you need to lighten up. Things can't be that bad." Kate, the everlasting optimist.

"I am depressing, aren't I?"

Kate snorted. "Didn't you guys kiss and make up."

"No."

"That's your problem."

A reluctant smile curved Jenny's lips. "Any more advice Dr. Kate? You can't seem to fix things with Mike and you want to tell me what to do?"

"I know." Her voice grew quiet. "It's just that things have never been right since Alex."

Jenny wrapped the phone cord around her ring finger. Kate hardly ever mentioned her one true love and when she did, it broke Jenny's heart.

Within minutes, Kate's teasing tone returned. "Listen, meet me for lunch and we'll compare notes. After all, isn't that what best friends are for?"

After agreeing on a meeting place, Jenny hung up, staring across the kitchen. Maybe Kate was right about lightening up. She'd been too serious since the break up with John. She wanted fun, not another heavy duty relationship. Nick had been providing that, until last night.

She took a sip of her lukewarm coffee. Maybe she should give them another chance. Maybe they could get back the magic of their friendship.

Right. And someone has a bridge to sell me.

She took her time getting dressed. Just as she was ready to leave, the doorbell rang. Despite her intentions not to get hung up on Nick, she hoped it was him. Instead, a young man holding a long, slim box with a huge red bow stood on her doorstep.

"Miss Meyer?"

She nodded.

"Delivery for you," he said, handing her the box.

She ran into the kitchen, dropped the box on the

table, and tore it open. Inside lay a dozen perfect red roses. With shaky hands she pulled out the card.

READY FOR LESSON NUMBER FIVE? YOU PLAN IT. N.

She laughed, a mingling of relief and joy. He wasn't giving up on them. So neither would she.

"Hurry, Nick, we're late!" Jenny tugged at his arm, dragging him across the parking lot.

"Jenny, what are we doing in a mobile home park?"

"It's part of our date. I can't explain right now, you'll find out."

Nick stopped abruptly. "I want to know before we go any further."

"You like spontaneity, so be surprised."

"Jenny." A warning, not an endearment.

"Okay, okay," she fumed. "The last couple of dates have been very . . . educational. When you asked me to plan this one, I wanted it to be special, to show you I'm an exceptional student."

"And the catch?"

She cleared her throat. "Well, things sort of got changed last minute."

"So this is it?" he asked, humor lacing his voice as he glanced around the lot. "I don't mean to be critical, but this doesn't seem very romantic. And we're defiantly over dressed to hanging out in a parking lot."

True. She wore a sleeveless black sheath dress and

spike heels, he wore a dark suit and tie. And they stood in the middle of a sand and crushed shell parking lot.

"Let me finish. My grandmother called and asked for a favor. She said to put on a fancy dress, which I did, I'm an obedient child." She looked him over from head to toe. "And you're wearing a suit, like I asked. Besides, I can't refuse her a thing, so here we are."

"What thing couldn't you refuse?"

She stood straight and smiled. "We are going to chauffeur four retired couples to a dinner cruise, stay with them for a few hours, then bring them home."

Nick shook his head, obviously disappointed. "Jenny, Jenny, Jenny. After all I've taught you, this is the best you could do?

"Nick, don't be so quick to judge. You'll have a great time, I promise. These folks have more life in them than some of my friends. Besides, it's different. Definitely something *you've* never done before."

He chuckled. "You got me there." He looked out over the park. "I don't know . . ."

"Look, the last man in the group to have his drivers license just got it revoked. Something about a tree in the middle of the road. Anyway, they're stuck here unless we help."

He grinned.

"Come inside and meet them." she urged, yanking him again. Her sandaled feet wobbled as they wended their way over the sandy lot. "You'll see."

The four couples descended upon them as soon as

Jenny pulled Nick into the community room. She quickly made introductions, allowing them time to get acquainted before leaving.

"So, Jennifer, this is the handsome young man you were telling me about."

"Yes, Gramma." Jenny averting Nick's gaze, hoping he'd miss her telling blush.

"Has he gotten serious yet?" Gramma asked in a stage whisper.

"Gramma, please."

"Tell me, son," Jenny's grandfather asked. "Do you have any problems driving at night?"

"No, sir." Nick arched an eyebrow in Jenny's direction. She smiled wanly and shrugged her shoulders.

"Good thing," the older man continued. "These duffers can't see a thing in broad daylight, let alone at night. That's why Jenny asked you along, to make sure we get where we're going in one piece. Hate to have such a small thing like Jenny driving the van around."

"The park has a van residents can use for outings like this," Jenny explained.

"Are you sure it's legal for me to drive it?"

"Oh, sure," another man called out. "We have permission to let our relatives drive. Have insurance and everything. Say, do you have a good driving record? Don't want you messing up our deal here."

"Now, now," the man's wife tapped his arm. "Look at Nick. He seems well behaved. How could a friend of Jennifer's be a bad driver? Have you known any of her friends to be wild?"

"There is that redhead," her husband replied.

"Kate's not wild, just enthusiastic," Gramma defended.

This comment created a discussion on youth today, and the merits of having a serious young man drive the van.

Jenny let them argue, realizing it was hopeless to get a word in. Nick grabbed her arm and drew her off to the side, away from the commotion.

"So, you don't have any wild friends?" Amusement twinkled in his gray eyes. "Maybe I should do something outrageous just to give them something to talk about."

"Don't encourage them. Besides, Mr. Cooper would probably join you." She cringed at the thought. Eight retirees and one single male causing havoc in Clearwater. It didn't bear thinking about.

"Have you filled your grandmother in on our dating lessons?"

"Not exactly. I told her we were dating, but left out the deal about you being my teacher. I don't think she'd understand."

"Hmm. So I'm supposed to be your boyfriend."

She grimaced. How embarrassing to be caught in a predicament like this. "If you wouldn't mind. It's just this one night."

Nick ran his finger over her cheek. "Actually, I wouldn't mind at all," he told her, his voice low and husky.

Jenny instantly turned warm, both his touch and his

words stroking a fire in her that flared to life. She looked into the depths of his eyes, mesmerized by the moment. His gaze lowered to her lips. Desire shivered through her when she remembered the delight of his kisses. She parted her lips in anticipation for just that, when her grandfather's voice startled her.

"Come on, you two love birds. We've got a dance floor to burn up. You can carry on with that stuff later."

Jenny felt a blush rush from the roots of her hair to her toes. What had gotten into her, to forget she was in the same room as her grandparents? It had to be Nick. He had that effect on her.

She glanced at Nick and had to stifle a giggle. He'd turned as red as she had. "Well, well, Coach. The old folks got to you, too."

"Not as much as you do."

She beamed at his compliment.

The oldsters hustled them outside and once everyone got settled, they took off. Nick concentrated on the driving, leaving Jenny to wander off in her thoughts.

She never lost control of herself with John, but she responded so physically to Nick's touch. When she knew they were going to see each other, she got so excited her stomach fluttered and a silly grin curved her lips. They teased, talked, and he cared about what she said and did. Funny, she never thought about John as a friend one way or the other, but she valued Nick's friendship. She'd really come to care about Nick, but beyond that? She thought she'd loved John and she'd been mistaken. Would she really know love when it was the real thing?

She knew she didn't believe in love at first sight. Affection, attraction, sure, but love? With Nick?

Earlier, when he looked into her eyes, he'd seemed more intense, more . . .

"A penny for your thoughts."

Jenny jumped.

Nick chuckled. "Must have been very interesting."

"Yes, well," Jenny stuttered, guilty of thinking about love. "Oh, look. We're here."

"You aren't getting out of this one so easily," Nick informed her. "I want to know what's going on in that mind of yours."

No you don't, she thought. He'd run, screaming for the hills if he had a clue. "Don't hold your breath," she teased as she climbed out of the van, slamming the door to emphasize her point.

Nick laughed loudly.

The couples assembled next to the van, eyes focused on Nick. His questioning gaze met hers. She stepped forward, handing him a small envelope.

"Here's the money for the tickets. You have to go up to the window and purchase them." She pointed to the small building at the entrance to the pier.

"That's part of my job, too?"

"Yes. They want you to feel you're part of the group. Oh, there's enough money to cover our tickets, too."

"No way," he argued. "You're my date for the evening. I'll take care of it."

"Please, Nick. It's their way of saying thank you for driving. They'd be hurt if you refused."

He shook his head and walked away, but to Jenny's relief he didn't argue about the money.

Once the passengers were on board, the ship cast off, traveling at a slow pace through the channel. Jenny stood on the deck, her loose hair blowing gently around her face. With a contented sigh, she basked in the last rays of sunlight before the twilight gave way to night.

Nick stood behind her and rested his hands on her bare shoulders. His fingers played with the straps, brushing her skin, leaving tingling trails of pleasure. Her heart hammered wildly inside her.

"That group of yours found a table near the dance floor. They said something about bogeying all night."

"I told you they were a lively bunch." She glanced over her shoulder at his piercing gray eyes, darkened now by the shadows of the setting sun. He had a puzzled expression on his face.

"What did your grandmother mean when she told me I was more than welcome to drive next time?"

Twisting around, Jenny braced the small of her back against the railing, a smile hovering on her lips as she peered over Nick's shoulder at the couples she loved. "My grandparents and their friends go out every other month. Each time they ask a different grandchild to come along. Lately, they've asked me more often. I guess they think I'm lonely since the breakup and it's their duty to cheer me up." The thought made her heart swell with love for her grandparents. "I go along because I like being with them."

"So if I'm your boyfriend, I'm invited too?"

"You got it."

Nick grinned. "They're something."

"Would you believe they've all been married for at least fifty years each? I watch my grandparents sometimes and I'm amazed at how sweet and caring they still are with each other. I think they love each other more today than when they first married."

"It almost makes you have faith in the institution of matrimony."

Brushing his lapels with her fingers, Jenny teased, "Nick, don't tell me you might convert to the lasting relationship theory."

"Don't get all excited. It's just a theory."

Jenny saw something she interpreted as regret in the gray depths before Nick blinked and it was gone. He sure could be stubborn.

After the sun set, the staff lit candles at the tables, a signal that dinner would be served. Nick held Jenny's chair out for her as they were seated. Ever the gentleman, she thought, smiling up at him.

The old folks rushed them through dinner, talking about nothing but dancing. Once the waiters began to clear the tables, the band started a set of swing music. She watched in awe as the dancers moved effortlessly around the floor, her light-footed grandparents included.

When the tempo slowed, Nick held his hand out to

her, escorting her to the dance floor. Swaying to a classic tune while nestled in his arms was pure heaven. She rested her head on his shoulder, inhaling his tangy cologne and reveling in the press of his strong body next to hers. He stroked her neck, sending chills of pleasure down her spine.

"I'm enjoying myself," he whispered into her ear, his breath fanning over the curve of her ear. She closed her eyes, enjoying an intense wave of pleasure.

The sudden clapping drew Jenny out of her dreamy haze. For a stunned moment she thought the applause came for her and Nick, as if everyone knew how he made her feel. When she focused on the inhabitants of the room, she realized the band was bowing before taking a short break.

Clearing her throat, she took an unsteady step backward. Nick watched her intently until she smiled. He took her hand, silently leading her back to the table. After glimpsing the smoldering fire in his eyes, she couldn't have spoken a coherent word even if she wanted to.

The waiters served desert with a flourish, but Jenny, too jarred by her emotions, declined to indulge. Instead, she happily listened to the conversation around the table.

"So, tell me you two, when do you plan on tying the knot?" Her grandfather fixed a serious gaze on Nick.

His sudden question made Jenny want to disappear. To be more specific, to crawl into a hole and hide.

"I beg your pardon?" Nick asked, turning pale.

"Well, with the way you two were going at it on the dance floor, I just assumed you were serious."

Jenny's mouth gaped open. Embarrassment kept her from uttering a word.

"Now don't tell me you plan on living together first," her grandfather continued. "Can't say I much agree with that kind of lifestyle you kids find acceptable today. In my day, when you met the right woman, you courted her, asked her daddy for her hand, then married her all proper like."

Opinions flew around the table as the couples gave their ideas on the state of marriage today. Jenny refused to look at Nick, afraid that he might be angry with her grandfather's remarks.

The band members returned, announcing the next set would be a waltz. When the ladies heard that Nick had never learned that dance, they argued over who would teach him.

"He's my granddaughter's beau, so that give me first dibs. Come along, Nick. The band awaits."

Jenny grabbed Nick's arm before he stood. "You can't waltz?"

"It's not something you learn everyday," he replied with a shrug. "I know how to slow dance and can manage some faster modern dancing, but who waltzes these days?"

"They do. Enjoy," she cried as her grandmother pulled him to the floor. They swirled around a few times, with Nick stumbling over his feet. When he passed by the sixth time, he mouthed, "Help me!"

She joined him, cutting in on her dear grandmother. After a few minutes, she had to admire the way he took direction when she instructed him on the finer points of the dance.

His fingers tightened at her waist as they swirled. "I thought you couldn't dance."

"You didn't ask me to waltz. Besides, there are some things I learned before I met you, Coach."

He swept her around the room. "Sometimes you surprise me."

She grinned. "See you don't know everything. You may fish better than me, but I'll pit my waltzing abilities against yours anytime."

He captured her gaze with his, the sultry light in his eyes making her warm, setting her heart racing. Even in a crowded room it was as though only the two of them inhabited the dance floor. She licked her dry lips as her gaze swept over his lips, then she returned his stare.

"Let's get some fresh air," he suggested. On the way out, they passed Jenny's grandfather who shot Nick a serious frown. Jenny guessed it must be some sort of secret signal between the men.

"Should I ask what that was all about?"

Nick led her to a quiet corner on the deck, away from prying eyes and loud music. "Just your grandfather's way of keeping me on the straight and narrow."

"Hmm." She stared up at the sparkling sky. "Did it work?"

"No way."

He gathered her into the circle of his arms, his head descending to hers for a slow kiss that immediately drugged her senses and did away with her ability to think rationally.

Ending the kiss, he cupped her face in his hands looking down at her with sleepy eyes. "I don't know what's gotten in to me tonight," he whispered in a husky voice. "I can't seem to get enough of you." He scattered kisses on her forehead, burying his face in her hair.

She tried to answer, but all she managed was a sigh that drifted to him as a whisper of warm breath on his cheek. Her fingers tips followed, outlining his mouth, his eyebrows.

"You shouldn't do that," he moaned. "We'd better stop before your grandfather catches us and forces you to marry me."

She grinned. "You make that sound like a bad thing."

He rested his forehead against hers and chuckled. "I've created a monster."

"You're lucky that I'm a model student. I always did enjoy extra credit work."

Shaking his head, he clasped her hand in his and headed for the dining room, stopping before the threshold. "I never expected our lessons to turn out quite like they have. Most of the time I feel like the student, learning about life through you. The way you care about those old folks and your family. It makes me believe in things I'd lost a long time ago." He smiled into her wide eyes. "I value our friendship and I do want more, but to be honest, I can't see beyond that."

She swallowed back the painful sting of rejection as he spoke the plain truth. Not that she should be surprised. He'd been completely honest with her from the start.

"I can't be more to you than just a teacher."

"Then I guess we should enjoy the lessons while they last. Once I graduate into the dating world, we won't be meeting like this."

Chapter Eight

Once I graduate, we won't be meeting like this.

The words echoed in Nick's head. He couldn't get them or Jenny's expression out of his mind. She'd been serious about using her new dating skills. His gut clenched at the thought.

If he was honest with himself, he'd admit he was more than 'just interested' in Jenny. Somewhere along the lessons, he'd grown fond of her. Okay, more than fond. Attracted. Deeply attracted. He was afraid she'd go off with another guy before he had a chance to find out what their relationship entailed.

All he knew was that he didn't want the lessons to stop. Because that meant not seeing Jenny.

Shaking his head, Nick stared down at the closed file folder marked, 'Chandler Corporation.' The meeting

had just ended and he was pleased that things had gone
well, better than he'd expected. The head honcho himself, Mr. Chandler, attended. After a round of hand-
shaking and small talk, Nick took the lead and pre-
sented the reasons why these men should choose
Bryson, Inc. exclusively for their building project. It
hadn't taken much to convince the group. Nick figured
they'd already made their decision and the meeting was
a formality.

It wasn't until after the formal meeting that things
got a bit . . . sticky. Nick jumped from his leather chair
and paced across the thick carpet in his private office.
When Mr. Chandler asked about family, Nick knew he
was in for it. He'd done enough research on the group
to know they were conservative, reliable, and old fashioned. Their philosophy was—a stable man respected
responsibilities, a dependable man saw a job through, a
married man is a happy man. Hadn't Chandler repeat-
ed that motto at least three times during the meeting?

Okay, so the guy had made his point. And for some
strange reason, Nick hadn't been as resistant as usual to
the idea that marriage could make a man happy. Not
that marriage was in the cards for him, but he wasn't
turned off by the conversation. So when Chandler had
asked him if he would be bringing a date the Parade of
Homes banquet, Nick said yes. He specifically told the
man that he was bringing his girlfriend, Jenny.

"Do I know her?" Chandler had asked.

"She works for the Nelson Design Group."

"An interior designer, correct? I believe we've used her firm before."

While Chandler had beamed at the news that Nick had a girlfriend, Nick found irony at the corner he'd talked himself into.

He needed a date with his girlfriend. He didn't have a girlfriend. The woman he was tutoring was not his girlfriend, yet Nick couldn't stop thinking how great it would be if she was. And now he had to ask Jenny to be his guest, no, his girlfriend, to save face. What a total mess.

He'd thought about asking Jenny to the banquet when he first bought the tickets, but since he'd been keeping his distance after their last date, he never asked.

Coward, his inner voice taunted. Yeah, maybe he was. But now he had to ask her. He was committed.

He stopped pacing and tilted his head back to gaze at the ceiling. He was in serious trouble here. He'd thought more about Jenny these past few weeks than he'd spent thinking about any of the other women he'd dated in the past. And the fact that he wanted to kiss her every time they were together, well, that was telling enough. He wasn't the kind of guy who easily shared his affection with women. He knew that once you kissed a woman, they started expected more out of a relationship. Expected more out of him.

But Jenny was different. What had started out as a novelty had changed for him. He found that he wanted more than lessons with Jenny. For the first time in his life, Nick wanted to be exclusive with one woman alone and she was thinking about dating other men.

Talk about a mess.

Pieces of raffia and palm lay strewn about the kitchen table. Frowning in concentration, Jenny deftly handled the natural materials. Basket weaving always helped her to relax. She'd mastered the craft just out of college and enjoyed it ever since. Not a birthday or Christmas passed without a relative hoping for one of her creations. Taking bits of straw and putting them together to form an original design made her feel in control. Something she seemed to be losing lately.

She hadn't spoken to Nick in a few days, and it was just as well. She'd been thinking a lot about their lessons. And the jumbled emotions that went with them. The dates had been successful. She was beginning to think it was time to move on her own if she ever hoped to find Mr. Right.

After that last date, she wondered if Nick could ever be the man for her. The one thing she couldn't fight was his past. And apparently Nick had a doozy. So for now they would remain friends, she would be there if he needed a sounding board, someone to talk with about his family. Because she really wanted him in her life.

She wrinkled her nose in disgust. Friendship with a man was vastly overrated.

So when Brad Reynolds, a realtor her firm worked with, asked her out, she said yes.

Granted, she hadn't heard bells and whistles when he asked her, but she did like him. He was attractive, ambitious and had connections. What more could a girl ask for?

Don't think about Nick. Don't think about how he'll react when you tell him.

So she smiled, said yes to Brad, set a date and tried her best to ignore the sinking sensation in her stomach. Then came home to make baskets and take her mind off her dilemma.

Just before six o'clock, the doorbell rang. Distracted by the intricate design she'd been working on, it took her a few minutes to put down the basket. The bell sounded again.

"I'm coming," she yelled, jogging to answer the door. Her stomach dipped when she viewed Nick standing on the other side and she tried not to sound overly excited. "Hi."

He grinned and looked her up and down. "Mind if I come in?"

"Of course not." She stepped back to let him pass, running her fingers through her tangled hair.

Nick grasped her hand. "Don't, you look perfect."

She kept her hand in his, curious about his unexpected visit. Judging by his striped shirt and dark slacks, he must have stopped here on the way home from work. "Let me guess. Another impromptu date?

Sorry," she glanced down at her T-shirt, shorts and bare feet. "Not dressed for the occasion."

He steered her into the living room and motioned for her to take a seat on the sofa before joining her. A lazy smile formed on his finely sculpted lips as he extracted a piece of raffia from her tangled hair. "Been rolling in the hay without me?"

She laughed, grabbing the straw from his fingers and twirling it between her own. "No, I was making a basket."

"A what?"

"It's a hobby."

"A messy one, I see."

"You should see the kitchen table."

He smiled politely, but Jenny could see he had something on his mind. She waited, curious and almost afraid to hear what he had to say. If he wanted to cancel their lessons or break up, why couldn't he do it over the phone like most men she'd heard Kate complain about?

"I had the meeting with the investors today." His voice offered no hint of good news.

Her heart sank. "What happened?"

"I got the deal."

She reached over to hug him, quickly, then sat back. "That's marvelous. I'm so happy for you."

He shifted one long leg out before him. "Yeah, it's great. But I have a problem."

Jenny tilted her head and frowned. "What is it?"

"I told Mr. Chandler that I was attending the Parade of Homes banquet with my girlfriend."

Her heart sank. If that were the case, why was he here rubbing her nose in that fact? "And?"

"So I'm here to ask my girlfriend to the banquet."

She opened her mouth, closed it, and blinked her eyes. "I'm sorry, I think I have some straw in my ears. Would you repeat that?"

He chuckled. "Mr. Chandler is a very conservative, everyone-should-be-happily-married kind of guy. So he likes stability in the people he works with. When he asked if I was going to the banquet and who I was taking, I said you."

"But I'm not your girlfriend."

"Technically. But we have been dating."

"No, we've had lessons."

"Semantics. Bottom line, we've been going out together for a while. That constitutes a friend. You're a girl. So what do you say? Will you go to the banquet with me?

She sank back against the cushions, stunned. Her head suddenly started pounding. *Now* he wanted her to be his girlfriend?

"Um, I would but I'm already committed to going to the banquet."

His brows angled down. "With whom?"

"With work, actually. Some of the designers are up for awards so the entire Nelson Group is going."

"Oh."

If she wasn't so confused, she'd laugh at his crest-fallen expression. She suspected most women didn't give up a date with Nick Bryson.

Tapping her finger across her lips, a plan formed in Jenny's mind. She should be locked up for considering this, but she'd been doing a lot of abnormal things late-ly, the majority of them with Nick.

"How about this," she started. "We'll go with our respective groups, but we can work the room together. That way, if Mr. Chandler stops you, we can be intro-duced."

"What if he sees us at different tables?"

"We just explain that for the award ceremony, we wanted to stay with our firms. In case we win. You know, solidarity and all that."

Nick thought about that for a moment. "He would go for that. He likes loyal employees."

"We'll just hook up whenever we aren't seated at the table."

"It could work." He didn't seem convinced, or happy with her proposal.

"What do you mean, it could. It's a brilliant idea."

The creases on his forehead disappeared, his eyes were still wary. "Yeah, it is. Thanks."

"Then I guess it's a date. Sort of."

"Yes, it's a date." Despite his obvious frustration, he flashed her a smile. "So, want to show me how you make a basket. You know, in case anyone ever asks?"

"Oh, I'm sure you get that all the time." She led him

to the kitchen, forcing her voice to high-pitched frequency. "Nick, please show me your baskets."

"It's better than asking someone to see my etchings."

She grinned. "Then step this way, Mr. Bryson."

"I'm in a jam," Jenny told Kate a few hours later, barely able to contain her panic. "Talk me through."

Kate laughed over background noise. "I doubt it, but fill me in."

"I accepted a date with Brad Reynolds. How do I tell Nick?"

"Hold on there. You're going out with another guy?"

"Yes."

"Why would you do that?"

Jenny paused for a moment, confused by the question. "That was the whole point. For me to start dating again."

"But you have Nick."

"Yeah, as my coach. Not as a real date."

"Hold on."

Jenny could hear music and laugher fade on the other end.

"Sorry, I had to go outside so I could hear you."

"I didn't mean to bother you."

"You aren't. This party is boring. Now, back to your problem. As I see it, you can't let Nick go."

Jenny blew out a frustrated puff of air. "I'm not letting him go. He was never mine to let go."

"Beside the point. You do have him."

"Earth to Kate. Get real here."

"I am. Look, he couldn't keep his eyes off you the other night. I'm telling you, he's hooked."

"If that's the case, he's failed to tell me."

"Give him time."

"Well, I don't have time. I decided to accept a date. I gave my word. All I want from you is advice, not a pep talk on Nick."

Kate sighed into the phone. "Fine. When do you see Nick again?"

"At the Parade of Homes banquet."

"Oh, goody. I get to be there for the fireworks."

"Kate—"

"Okay, okay. Here's my advice. Tell him just before you end the evening, then close the door real quick."

"That's it?"

"Yep. And don't mention this was my idea."

Chapter Nine

By the night of the banquet, Jenny was a bundle of nerves. She'd spoken to Nick a few times on the phone, mainly to get their game strategy down for tonight. Things had been going well until Kate called and mentioned her other date.

"Brad will probably be there, you know."

Jenny hadn't thought of that, but it made sense. They were all in the same line of work one way or another. Great, like she needed more pressure.

What really bothered her is that she felt like she was cheating on Nick. Which was foolish, considering they weren't really together. She had the right to date anyone, just as Nick did. But it bothered her. And she knew why. Her feelings for Nick had zoomed past coach and friend to romance and happily ever after.

"Not in this lifetime," she muttered, putting the finishing touches on her makeup. She pulled her hair up and secured it with a jeweled barrette. Tendrils curled around her face. Smiling at the results, she went to her bedroom to finish dressing.

She'd chosen a strapless, shimmery, pink chiffon dress with a double tier flounce skirt. It fell to her calves, the perfect length to show off a pair of slinky, spiky sandals.

She'd just finished with the sparkly earrings and necklace when the doorbell rang. Taking a deep breath, she hurried to the door.

"Hi," she said as Nick stood at her threshold, looking very handsome and debonair in a dark suit. The white shirt contrasted to his tanned skin. He said nothing, just stared at her with hooded eyes. She wanted to fidget under his enigmatic gaze but silently kept her poise.

"Ready?" he finally asked, his tone husky.

"Sure let me get my wrap and bag."

She walked to the hall table to collect her things, then stepped out into the warm spring evening.

"I have a favor to ask," Nick said after he had them settled in his Corvette.

"Okay."

"I have to swing by a job site before we go to the banquet. Do you mind?"

"No. Last minute emergency?"

"You could say that. Mike called about fifteen minutes ago. The crew ran into a snafu. They need the boss for a final decision."

"Take your time," she told him as the sports car rumbled toward the work site.

Shortly, they pulled up to a house under construction. About five workmen lingered in the open garage, while Mike, the foreman on the job, strode to the car.

Nick reached over and squeezed her hand. "Be right back."

Jenny leaned forward in the seat to view the house. Although partially constructed, she could visualize the final product. If Nick had designed it, he couldn't have come any closer to her dream house than this. How weird was that? It's as if he looked into her mind and saw the type of house she'd always wanted. She shook her head. He'd designed this long before meeting her. But still . . . chills danced over her.

On impulse, she opened the door and cautiously stepped into the dirt. She didn't want to ruin her new sandals, but she couldn't resist taking a closer look.

Her dress whipped up in the breeze, dancing around her legs and causing a few raised eyebrows from the crew. She ignored them, taking small steps around the scattered debris until she reached the open door. As she stepped inside, her stomach lurched. How perfect was this?

Taking a self-appointed tour, she went from room to room, marveling at the design. As she wandered, she lost herself in her artists mind, working up mental plans to finish the interior.

The men suddenly clamored into the kitchen area, so

Jenny decided to return to the car. She pulled her skirt tightly around her, keeping the hem from getting dusty.

Nick stood by the car as she approached, his arms crossed over his chest, an odd glint of concern in his eyes. "I thought I told you to stay in the car."

"I just wanted to look around. Don't worry, I was careful. The walls are still standing."

"That's not what I worried about. You could have been hurt."

"But I wasn't."

He hesitated for a moment. "So, what did you think?"

"It's great. I love the floor plan. There's so much space, so much to work with."

He grinned. "Glad you like it. I've been thinking that I might move in once it's completed."

"It'll be beautiful," she assured him.

Mike called for Nick from the front door. "I found the shipping order."

Nick glanced over her shoulder. "Be right there." Then he looked her straight in the eye. "Wait here. We'll be ready to leave in a minute."

"Promises, promises."

He kept true to his word and joined her within minutes.

"Isn't Mike going to the banquet?"

"No. Apparently he and Kate had a parting of the way, so he decided to skip tonight just in case she shows up."

"She'll be there, she told me so."

"Then it's a good thing Mike is working."

Once they reached the luxurious hotel that was hosting the banquet, Nick gave his keys to the valet and escorted Jenny inside. The cool air conditioning brushed over her skin. As she draped the wrap over her shoulders, she felt Nick's warm hands grab hold of the material and adjust the wrap over her arms. She shivered at his touch.

"Cold?" he asked.

Not really, not when her blood heated up every time he touched her. "Just fine."

They entered the banquet room to the sound of murmured voices and a string quartet playing classical music in the far corner. He led her to a corner bar where they both ordered a drink, then they milled around.

Along the walls on either side of the large room where displays of the different houses receiving awards. There were photo shots of the houses, as well as pictures of the interior design for the homes. Each firm represented was listed on the display.

"Look, Bryson Inc." She looked closely at the display. "Nick, this house is fabulous."

"Thanks. It was one of my more challenging jobs. The property is right on the water. The view is beautiful, but the piece of property was a nightmare to work on."

"It must have worked out. This committee doesn't just hand out awards, you have to earn it."

He took a sip of his drink but his eyes never left hers. She wondered what he was thinking.

They moved on, stopping by a display for a builder who had used the Nelson Design Group for the interior designs.

"One of your projects?" Nick asked. His hand rested on the small of her back and she almost lost her train of thought.

"Yes. I was in charge of most of the work."

"You have a good eye. I like the design, clean and elegant at the same time."

Her chest filled with pride. "Thanks, Nick. That means a lot to me."

She glanced up at him to find his gaze meeting hers. Her body temperature rose and all sound around her muted. She leaned into him, an involuntary motion that was becoming second nature to her. His fingers tightened at her waist and he started to speak when a booming voice sounded behind them.

"Nick."

Jenny nearly jumped back, so startled by the intrusion in her private world with Nick. He removed his hand and turned.

"Mr. Chandler," he said, putting emphasis on the name as he introduced her.

Jenny frowned, then remembered this was the man Nick wanted her to meet. She shook of the seductive languor from Nick's touch and put on her party face.

"So pleased to meet you," she told the older man as she shook his hand. "Nick has told me so much about you."

"But he hasn't said much about you, my dear."

"Nick tends to hold things close to the vest."

"Very true. I'm glad to meet the woman who could steal Nick's heart."

She felt herself blush. "I don't know about that," she murmured.

"I do. I'm rather an expert on these things." Mr. Chandler winked at her and she wanted to excuse herself and escape.

"Now then, I noticed you two looking over this display. Yours?" he asked her.

"My design firm did the work on this home."

Chandler viewed the pictures for a good few minutes before turning to Nick. "I like it. I want you to get Jenny here to do the design work on our model home."

"I'm not sure Jenny can work—"

"Nonsense. Offer her firm the job. I'll add an additional sum to our contract in order to secure her talent." He beamed at Jenny. "It's been a pleasure. I'll leave you and Nick to the details."

The businessman sauntered off, leaving behind a speechless Jenny. She snuck a peek at Nick, growing wary at the frown on his face.

"Nick, we don't have to work together. I understand if you want to pass."

"You heard the man. He usually gets what he wants. He wants you."

As Nick said the words, his eyes glittered with a hidden emotion Jenny couldn't decipher. All she knew was that she wished Nick wanted her.

The crowd had grown thicker since they arrived and soon it was time to take their seats for dinner. Just before they parted to go to their separate tables, Brad Reynolds stopped beside Jenny.

"Still on for Friday?" he asked.

She swallowed hard, trying to ignore Nick's pointed stare.

"Yes."

"See you at seven."

Brad took off, leaving her standing by Nick, feeling uncomfortable and guilty.

"Plans?" he asked.

"Um, actually I have a date."

One eyebrow rose. "Were you going to tell me?"

"Eventually." She took a deep breath. "I wanted to see if your lessons would work."

"Good luck then," he said before turning on his heel, heading to his table.

"Great, just great," she muttered, knowing she'd ruined any more lesson dates with Nick.

"I'm not comfortable with this," Nick told Kate three nights later as they sat in his Corvette outside Sparky's, a local hangout that featured loud music.

"Don't give up on Jenny now," Kate admonished. "She needs you to rescue her, you know, like a knight in shining armor. Trust me, Brad's a player. He's no good for her."

And I am? Nick shook his head. "She's not going to like this."

"She'll be fine once she knows why you're here."

"Remind me, exactly, why I'm here."

"To sabotage Jenny's date."

"Right. She's not going to be happy with us."

"You said that already." Kate opened the door, placing one foot on the asphalt before she turned to him. She wore a pair of faded low-rise jeans and a small T-shirt. He'd dressed much the same, jeans and a polo shirt. "Just follow my lead."

Nick pocketed his keys and followed the lively redhead into Sparky's. He really knew Jenny wouldn't appreciate their interference, yet when Kate called him and proposed this crazy idea, he couldn't refuse. It wasn't that he thought Jenny was incapable of taking care of herself; he didn't want her out with any other guys. Period.

With a rueful smile he acknowledged the truth. He'd changed his tune about relationships since he met Jenny. His life would never be the same.

They entered the lively atmosphere just as the band started another set.

"Do you see her?" Kate yelled over the music.

Nick shook his head, not bothering to be heard over the music. He figured it wouldn't take Kate very long to find their quarry.

After one circuit around the room, Kate turned to him, brows drawn together. "I don't see them."

Nick noticed a door leading outside and tilted his head in that direction. Kate followed his lead and soon they were on the patio. Dim lighting from the muted overhead lights and twinkle lights wrapped around the railings of the deck formed a romantic ambiance. Nick really hoped Jenny and her date weren't nestled in a corner somewhere. As far as he was concerned, Jenny had been a deft pupil. There was no telling what might happen on a night like this.

Kate grabbed his arm, her fingers digging into his biceps. "There they are."

He followed her gaze. Sure enough, at a secluded table in the far corner of the patio sat Jenny and the date. She looked fantastic in a simple, sleeveless dress. Her hair shined in the soft lighting and her skin glowed. When his heart rate picked up, he grinned. Only Jenny had this affect on him.

Her date seemed to be telling her a story, but he noticed she kept looking down at her glass. His mood lifted. Things might not be so bad after all.

Kate dragged him toward the couple. "Hey, girl-friend," she called out. Jenny's head snapped up at the sound of her friend, but her eyes grew wide with sur-prise when she spotted Nick.

"Nick? Kate? What are you two doing here? Together?"

"We were both dateless," Kate explained, "so we decided to go out. I can't believe we ran into you."

Jenny's eyes narrowed at Kate. "I told you I'd be here."

"Did you? Must have slipped my mind."

Jenny opened her mouth as if to say something, then though better of it.

"Nick, let's join them." Kate already pulled a vacant chair to the table, all the time grinning at Brad. He seemed confused at first, but after the introductions, focused on the redhead.

Nick found another chair nearby and dragged it over, next to Jenny. She didn't exactly glare at him, but she didn't look too pleased.

"Care to explain?" she asked in a low voice.

"Kate had an idea."

She glanced at her friend and back. "And you went along with it?"

Shaking her head, she stood, took his hand and marched them down the steps and around the building, stopping under a bright light in the parking lot. She placed her hands on her hips. "I warned you about Kate."

"The girl doesn't take no for an answer. I admit it, she talked me into coming here. Now I'm wondering how mad you are and if it was worth it."

"Kate does have a way of manipulating people."

"So does that mean you aren't royally ticked off?"

"Depends. Tell me why you're really here."

He ran a hand through his hair. "I was hoping your date would be a disaster."

"Because . . . ?"

"I'm jealous, okay?"

"You are?"

He shifted his stance, uncomfortable with this soul-bearing stuff. "Guilty as charged."

She grinned. "That was a very good answer."

"So I'm out of the dog house?" he asked, seeing a light at the end of this emotional tunnel.

"For now. Nick, I can take care of myself you know. There was no need to spy on me."

"We never spied. Kate is like a homing device. We found you right away."

"And I'm supposed to be flattered?"

"Jenny, I'm sorry. There's was no need for me to show up here."

She reached out and took his hand in hers. "I'm glad you did," she said softly.

"Because it was a bad date or because you missed me?"

"Both."

At least she was honest. Now he really felt like a heel. "Listen, I promise never to do this again. When you go out, it'll be you and your date. Alone. I swear."

"No need to go that far."

"I suppose—"

His cell phone rang, cutting off his words. He grudgingly let her warm hand go and unclipped the phone from his belt, reading the caller ID. His mother. Her third call of the night. "Do you mind if I take this?"

"No. Go ahead."

He answered with a terse hello.

"Nick, its Mother. I've been trying to reach you all week. Did you forget about the special dinner at the Breakers this coming weekend in honor of your father? You never sent your RSVP."

With all that had been going on, he'd forgotten about the party. "No. I hadn't decided if I was coming."

"I'm not one to beg, but this is really important to him. Please come home, if only to stay overnight."

Nick heard the plea in her voice and every muscle in

his body stiffened. He'd never heard Louisa use that tone before. It almost sounded as if she cared.

"Is it that big a deal?"

"Very."

He closed his eyes and took a deep breath. "I'll be there."

"Thank you," his mother said in a hoarse whisper before she ended the connection.

Hanging up the phone, Nick glanced at Jenny. "How would you like to try lesson number six: meeting the family?"

Chapter Ten

The late afternoon sun cast long shadows on the exclusive shops of Worth Avenue. From the passenger side of Nick's Corvette, Jenny scanned the sidewalks, watching the well dressed patrons stroll by.

"Want to stop and do some shopping?" Nick asked.

"No. I'd rather meet your family first," she replied, glad that Nick finally felt inclined toward conversation. He'd been quiet for most of the five hour drive, answering her questions with a minimum of words.

"We can take in the local sights tomorrow, unless the family has plans. If so, I'll make sure we can be by ourselves on Sunday," Nick offered.

"That's fine with me. I'd like to shop and see the Flagler Museum."

Nick nodded, steering through the exclusive downtown area. Shortly after they entered a residential area, and as they drove, Jenny admired the beautiful houses with well manicured lawns. To her disappointment, many were hidden behind tall privacy hedges or walls. Hissing sprinkler systems generously watered the rich grass and tropical plants that flourished in the humid South Florida climate. Inhaling deeply, she closed her eyes to enjoy the scent of the moist earth and blooming flowers.

Spring was giving way to summer. Longer days, soaring temperatures and unexpected storms would soon be upon them. She opened her eyes and adjusted her sunglasses as she peered into the sky. Scattered black rain clouds were already moving inland. There would definitely be a brief downpour as the rain clouds passed over them.

Nick pulled the car off the main road, driving a short distance to turn into a circular driveway. He stopped the car before a sprawling Spanish style house.

"Welcome to the homestead."

Jenny's stomach fluttered with nerves. When they left Clearwater she'd been anxious and each hour that drew them closer to Palm Beach had her jumpy with worry. Now they sat before his parent's home, with Jenny as tense as Nick looked.

She started when Nick appeared at her door to help her out. He glanced at his watch. "Great timing. We're just in time for the Friday night meal. A dining experience one shouldn't miss."

The heavy sarcasm in his voice made her heart sad. She always enjoyed dinner with her family. Squaring her shoulders, she decided that no matter how grim Nick sounded, she was determined to make the best of this meal and the weekend.

Hopefully, being in the midst of his family would help shed some light on the problems he kept from her. She might be able to help him resolve this negative reaction toward his family.

Taking her hand, Nick led them up the steps to the ornate front door. In his jeans and sports shirt he looked like he just stepped out of *GQ*, as if he'd never left the privileged life. He didn't bother to knock, but entered the house as if he still lived there. His mother must have seen them drive the car up. She waited for them in the foyer.

"Nick, I'm so glad you made it home."

Standing before them stood a beautiful older woman. Dressed in a dove gray dress that complimented her dark hair and creamy completion, even her accessories matched perfectly. She realized where Nick got his good looks.

Jenny's confidence plummeted at the sight. Here she stood in wrinkled pink cotton shorts and tank top. She hated to think what her wind-blown hair must look like. So much for first impressions.

Louisa continued to gush all over Nick. "You made it in time for the family dinner. Your father is home and Valerie and Howard should be here any minute. Susan won't make it, she's getting another divorce, and—" she stopped in mid-sentence, noticing Jenny for the first time. Astute gray eyes focused on the grasp Nick had on Jenny's hand. Her soft drawl reflected her curiosity. "I'm so sorry. Here I am going on and on and I've practically ignored your guest. Are you going to introduce us?"

His narrow-eyed gaze, the same as his mother's, never left the woman's face as he said, "Jenny, this is my mother, Louisa Bryson. Mother, this is Jenny Meyer." He paused. "My girlfriend."

Louisa's hand fluttered to her throat as surprise colored her complexion. "My goodness. I wasn't aware that you were involved with anyone. I thought maybe you and Ashley . . ."

"No way." He shivered at the thought. "You know how I feel about her." He glanced at Jenny and grinned. "We've been seeing each other for a few weeks now."

Jenny reached out to take Louisa's hand. "I'm so pleased to meet you, Mrs. Bryson."

"Call me Louisa," she replied, smiling pleasantly. "Come into the living room and have a drink before dinner."

Louisa went on ahead of them but Jenny held Nick back.

"Why did she think this Ashley was coming?" she demanded on a tight whisper.

"I told her I was bringing someone on the night she called. We had a quick conversation, I never mentioned names. She just assumed it was Ashley."

"So why is this the first time I've heard about this girl?"

He grinned at her. "Jealous?"

Jenny glared at him.

He chuckled. "Ashley is the daughter of my mother's best friend. They've been hoping we'd get together for years."

"And you haven't?"

"She's not my type."

With that vague answer, they entered a spacious living room, tastefully decorated in ecru, peach, and sea foam green. The soothing tones calmed Jenny. She was fighting the temper that came from Nick's omission, as well as the surprise at his declaration that she was his girlfriend. It was hard enough to make a good first impression with the all these conflicting emotions swirling inside her.

Taking a deep breath, she sank into the soft sofa. Nick went to the bar to pour a cola for Jenny and a soda water for his mother. He popped the top off his soda before stretching out on the couch beside Jenny.

Louisa sipped her drink, gazing at Nick with a troubled expression. "Your father should be joining us any minute. He's dressing for dinner."

Which was why Louisa was dressed to the nines. Jenny figured Mr. Bryson would dress just as formally, as well as the rest of the family. Jenny turned to Nick, speaking through clenched teeth. "Why didn't you tell me they dress up for dinner?"

Nick swallowed his soda. "Slipped my mind, I guess. It's all part of the Bryson code."

"Great," she muttered.

An eyebrow lifted over amused eyes. "You'll be fine, no matter what you wear. Don't worry."

How could she not worry? This was her first time meeting his family. *She* wasn't expected, Ashley obviously was. She didn't bring very fancy clothes except for her dress for the banquet. What else could go wrong? As soon as they were alone, she was going to have words with Nick.

"Whatever you wear is fine," Louisa assured her. "Tell me, Nick, where did you meet Jenny?"

"He found me at the Sports Grille," Jenny answered before Nick could say a word.

Louisa raised her brow. "How interesting. And after he found you?"

"I bought him a drink, we talked and the next thing you know, we're dating."

"Just like that," Nick added, his lips curved at her story. "From one interesting date to another."

Louisa eyed them both, clearly curious as to their conversation, but obviously too polite to ask. "Well, I'm pleased for both of you. You make a lovely couple."

Gradually the tension ebbed from Jenny and she found herself grateful that Louisa obviously accepted Nick's explanation for her presence. With relief, Jenny realized that his mother wasn't as bad as Nick made her out to be.

Charles Bryson entered the room a short time later. "Nick. Great to see you, Son."

Nick stood and shook hands with his father. "You too, Dad."

Jenny rose, moving closer to Nick, nervous once again as she stared at the impressive man before her. Standing tall, with broad shoulders much like Nick, Charles had the physique of an athlete. Graying hair complimented his tanned skin and he resembled the stylish executive in a pair of dark slacks and a powder blue long sleeved shirt and patterned tie. He seemed unapproachable, as though he kept people at a distance, including his family.

"Charles, dear," Louisa interrupted, coming to stand beside her husband. "Nick has brought someone with him that he'd like you to meet."

"Really?" Charles frowned at Jenny. "I'm sorry, I didn't notice you, young lady."

Wonderful, Jenny thought. So much for a spectacular first impression.

Nick put his arm around Jenny in a casual fashion, but she felt the tension in his muscles. "Dad, I'd like you to meet Jenny."

Charles glanced at her, then at Nick. "I thought you were bringing Ashley?"

Jenny had to bite the inside of her cheek to keep her frustration from spilling out. What was it with these people and Ashley?

"No, Dad. Jenny and I have been dating for a while now."

Jenny swallowed and held out her hand to Charles. "Hello, sir."

Charles intentionally ignored her, turning instead to glare at his wife.

Louisa smiled weakly at her husband, then glanced at Nick. Her hands were clasped together and her voice was strained. "Isn't it just like our son to do something impulsive, then tell us afterward?"

"Who is her family?" His father pointedly asked Nick.

"She's from Clearwater. You don't know them."

"What does it matter?" his mother chimed in. "She's really a lovely young woman."

A commotion in the foyer momentarily drew the attention from Jenny as a couple floated into the room, dressed to the nines.

"My sister, Valerie, and her husband, Howard," Nick informed her under his breath.

"Hello, Daddy." Valerie glided across the room in a rustle of silk, a jangle of jewelry, and a scented trail of expensive perfume. She kissed her father's cheek, nodded curtly to Louisa, and smiled at Nick. Howard mimicked every move.

"Well, Nicky, what's new?"

"Still not married," came his dry reply.

Valerie's lips formed a thin line, as did Howard's, in comical timing. "Funny." She gazed at Jenny. "Who is she?"

"My date for Dad's dinner."

Jenny could imagine Valerie taking mental inventory of her wrinkled traveling clothes and lack of jewelry. Even if this was Nick's sister, she was hard pressed to be polite. "Nice to meet you."

"I don't recall ever seeing you around town," Valerie

muttered, her eyes narrowed as she looked Jenny up and down. "Do our families travel in the same circles?"

Jenny smiled over clenched teeth. This woman knew very well that they didn't frequent the same places. "I don't think so," she replied.

Valerie turned her attention to her father and his pained expression. "I suppose you've made Daddy unhappy, haven't you Nicky?"

"Be quiet, Valerie."

"Imagine, St. Nick, doing something wrong for a change."

Louisa frowned as she walked to Jenny, lightly touching her arm. "Why don't you and Nick change for dinner. We have about fifteen minutes before we sit down. I'll have Nina ready a room for you."

Jenny couldn't wait to get to the solitude of her own room. "Thank you."

"That's Mama, ever the hostess," Valerie announced, sarcasm lacing her voice. She retreated to the bar to talk to her father, Howard in tow.

Nick led Jenny to his old bedroom while they waited for Nina to prepare her room. His suitcase had already been deposited on a stand at the foot of the bed while hers sat in the hallway. An awkward stillness fell over them as Jenny waited for Nick to speak. Since he remained tight-lipped, she decided to break the silence.

"That seemed to go well."

With a heavy sigh, Nick flopped down on the bed, landing on his back. "Yeah, if you enjoy standing before a firing squad."

Laughing, Jenny sat down in a chair by the desk. Nick threw his arm over his eyes, whether shielding himself from the light or his family, she couldn't tell.

"So, am I the little secret that is supposed to upset the family apple cart?"

"No."

"Truth here, Nick."

He leaned up on his elbows. "Okay, maybe a little. I don't like it when I'm expected to be at their beck and call. I have a life away from them. One that includes you."

"I would have appreciated a heads up. Especially on this Ashley thing."

"I honestly had no idea they thought I'd bring her. Ashley and I grew up together, that's it. I've never thought of her as anything more than a little sister."

"Does she think of you as more than a brother?"

He shrugged. "I don't know. I bump into her from time to time because she runs her mother's boutique in Clearwater, but other than that we have different lives. I don't particularly like the crowd she hangs with."

"But your parents do."

"That's because it's the same type of friends they have." He sighed. "I told you that my father wants me back here, involved in his work. If I'm involved with a girl from their crowd, maybe he thinks I'll give in. But I won't. I've worked too hard to make my company successful."

"Well, that'll just make this weekend a little more interesting."

He stared at her for a long time. "Why didn't you get angry and ask me to take you home?"

"Because that's not how I operate. I'll make due."

"I'm really sorry, Jenny. I want you to have a good time."

"You did warn me that it wouldn't be easy meeting your folks. Your mother is lovely and your father, well, he's intimidating. Your sister . . . never mind. My mom always said if you don't have anything nice to say—"

When he looked at her, his eyes were troubled.

"You okay?" she asked softly.

"I don't care what they think, you know. You're my friend and I won't allow them to make you feel uncomfortable or unwelcome."

"Back to that again? Friend? I thought I was your girlfriend."

"Can't you be both?"

Could they be both? It's what she wanted, had for some time now. Instead of speaking, she smiled at the man she'd come to love, despite his difficult past.

And she knew for sure that she did love him. Maybe she had from the first time they met. It really didn't matter when it happened. She only knew that this romantic, last-forever, take-my-breath-away kind of love she had with Nick had never happened to her before. It was Nick alone, now and for always.

She went over to him, gently kissing him, hoping to distract him from his family for a few minutes.

"You know," he said, his lips playing over hers. "We

only have about five minutes left to get ready before dinner."

"Five what?" Caught up in the rush of desire at being close to Nick, she'd forgotten about dinner. Suddenly she realized what he was saying and rushed into hallway, nearly colliding with Nina. The older woman led Jenny to her room. Right next door to Nick's.

She closed her door on his laughter, trying hard to hold onto the mad she'd worked up about Nick not warning his parents that he'd invited her to be his guest. Now that she'd met everyone, she realized Nick hadn't told them about her on purpose. His way of throwing them off. Too bad she was the one at the short end of the stick.

Determined to make the best out of a bad situation, she familiarized herself with the room and adjoining bath. Very plush. Very elegant. Not at all homey.

Sighing, she hefted her suitcase onto the hope chest at the end of the double bed. She quickly chose a suitable outfit, knowing it fell far short of what Louisa and Valerie were wearing. In minutes, Nick would be knocking at her door to escort her to dinner.

She changed, fixed her hair and makeup. Shrugging, she realized she was as ready as she'd ever be.

Chapter Eleven

Before she even opened her eyes, the conscious feeling of being in a strange place wrapped around Jenny. Sighing, she lay on her back, holding the pillow close to her chest. The mid-morning sun filtered through the draperies. The alluring scent of fresh coffee served as her silent alarm clock. She stretched, feeling lazy and not in the least concerned about leaving her cozy haven.

Until she remembered where she was. Glancing at the clock, she realized she'd missed Nick before he left the house to play a round of golf with his father. She had plans to shop with Louisa.

While spending time shopping sounded appealing, it also meant time alone with Nick's mother. She seemed so nice, but Jenny had reservations about going off with her for the day. Nick's disdain for his mother was obvious and it had to come from something in their past. Problem was, she didn't have a clue what is was. Talk about being uncomfortable.

Last night she'd asked why Nick and his sister acted so unfriendly toward their mother.

"I guess you could say that the family is disappointed in my mother. She's done some things we can't forgive her for."

"That may be so, but it's clear that she adores you, Nick. I could see it the moment we walked in the door. She's excited that you're here and she's the only one who made me feel welcome. And her sense of humor really put me at ease."

Nick leaned against the wall, the moonlight bathing his somber face. "She does have a great sense of humor. When I was growing up she was always my confidante, my partner in crime. We were the best of friends," he looked away, "but that changed."

"Have things really changed that much?"

"Yes."

"Are you ever going to fill me in?"

But Nick didn't reply. Instead, he took her in his arms and made her forget the conversation. He certainly had a superior way of changing the subject, but Jenny felt the undercurrents stirring around them. She'd hoped this weekend would finally be the time Nick revealed his family problems.

Jenny sat up, realizing she had to get ready for a day of shopping. The dress she brought for the party wouldn't work. She needed a formal dress since the party they were attending tonight was at the Breakers. A local finance group Charles belonged to was honoring him on a special civic project he'd headed. And since she didn't think her choice was appropriate to wear, Louisa had offered to take her shopping.

Throwing back the covers, she shook away her dismal thoughts and padded across the plush carpet to retrieve her robe. A loud knock on the door startled her.

Louisa poked her head into the room. "Just wanted to check if you were ready to leave."

"I just need a few minutes to dress, then we'll shop till we drop."

Louisa took Jenny to Worth Avenue. The three blocks of prime real estate featuring exclusive boutiques and well known designer shops were a shoppers dream come true. Louisa stopped at the several boutiques, she knew well and encouraged Jenny to stop at the other stores whenever she pleased.

One shop drew particular interest for Jenny after Louisa told her that Nick used to frequent the place; a military antique shop containing everything from miniature toy soldiers to full dress uniforms, along with paintings, medals, and memorabilia.

"Nick collected toy soldiers," Louisa reminisced. "He belonged to a club of young men who set up mock battles. He'd plan his strategies for days before a 'skirmish,' as he put it. Every Christmas I would treat him to any item in the store, then we'd go home and he'd show me what his next battle entailed. I really enjoyed those times together."

"Does he still have the collection?" Jenny asked.

"Oh yes, a very extensive one. It's worth a great deal."

"I never realized he had an interest in military memorabilia."

"Since he was a boy. He was actually involved in all sorts of tournaments through the club. Now that he's grown, he seems to have forgotten how much time he put into his collection."

Jenny felt a pang of despair in the vicinity of her heart. One more part of Nick's life he hadn't shared with her. She realized that she couldn't know everything about him in the short time they'd been together, but it still bothered her.

Louisa must have noticed her discomfort when she asked, "Are you all right, dear?"

She quickly shed the depressing thoughts. "Yes, of course. I was thinking that maybe you could help me pick out a soldier for Nick. I'd like to get him a memento to remember this trip."

"I'd be delighted." Drawing Jenny into the store, Louisa led them to a display of intricately carved soldiers. They made their selection, then continued browsing in other store windows.

They stopped for lunch at a very elegant restaurant. Jenny marveled at Louisa's polish and ease in such posh surroundings. Even though she didn't frequent these types of places, she lost any nervousness that had surfaced earlier and enjoyed hearing about Nick's childhood. Nick's mother made her feel at ease and she appreciated the effort, but knew it wasn't enough. She didn't want his friends to look down on her as his sister had, and even went so far as to mention her concern to Louisa.

A silence fell between them as the older woman frowned before speaking her thoughts. "The one thing you must remember, Jenny, is that people are people. Some are easy to get along with, while with others you put on a smiling face and tolerate them." Her bitter chuckle revealed that she'd had her share of toleration. "Eventually you breathe a sigh of relief when you don't have to be socially correct any longer."

Once again she found herself wondering what this woman could have done to make her family despise her. She seemed so down to earth, working so hard to make a friend of Jenny. And she didn't have to try hard, Jenny truly liked her.

"I guess the though of meeting Nick's friends has me nervous."

Louisa patted her hand. "Just be you. I think my son is very lucky to have found a sweet woman such as yourself. Like me, he doesn't care if other people have lots of money or not. He chooses his companions by the wealth of their friendship, not the depth of their pockets."

"Well, that explains why he got involved with me."

A gentle laugh escaped Louisa's lips. "Don't worry about tonight."

"I can't help it. I want to find the perfect outfit, but I don't usually shop in exclusive boutiques."

"I have a wonderful idea." Louisa's face lit up. "I know the perfect store to find a dress. We'll go there first, then go have our hair and makeup done? A regular girl's afternoon out."

Jenny's heart nearly broke. How long, if ever, had it been since Louisa spent this kind of day with her daughters? Probably not since they were children.

Louisa watched her, anxiously trying to hide the importance of Jenny's answer. How could she refuse this woman? Her cheeks were bright and her eyes sparkled with pleasure. Before she knew it, she'd agreed.

Louisa steered Jenny to the Esplanade. The smaller mall had an old world charm to it, and housed branches of many designers from around the world. Jenny loved the Mediterranean style, the quiet walkways passing under arches that led to courtyards with fountains.

At Louisa's favorite designer shop, her couturier selected several dresses for Jenny to choose from. After much deliberation between the two women, Jenny settled on a midnight blue, sleek floor length, off-one-shoulder gown. It had to be the most elegant dress she'd ever dreamed of owning. She peered at herself in the mirror; she looked like a glamourous model. This outfit would raise Nick's eyebrows, she thought in flushed anticipation.

"With your blond hair and fair coloring, you look exquisite," the store owner gushed as Jenny joined them.

Louisa nodded in approval. "It's simple and simplicity is a valuable fashion statement, especially when compared to all flash with no substance."

Jenny accepted Louisa's compliment with pleasure. The woman had an inbred elegance about her that wasn't forced of fake, so Jenny felt secure that the woman had led her in the right fashion direction. Besides that, she loved it.

"I have some jewelry at home that will be perfect with the outfit. I can't wait until Nick sees you."

After purchasing the gown and accessories, they traveled to the hair salon where they were pampered for the remainder of the afternoon. The stylist swept Jenny's hair into a stylish French twist. Loose tendrils framed her face. The striking style left her slender neck exposed, an effect that would be dazzling with the cut of her gown.

Next, she had her makeup flawlessly applied by an expert. Jenny spent a good deal of time staring in the mirror, assuring herself that this new facade still held the same old Jenny. How easy it would be to become accustomed to this indulgent lifestyle, she mused.

When they moved to the nail table, Louisa regaled Jenny with stories of Nick's childhood as the technician polished their nails. From the funny anecdotes she told, Jenny knew that Louisa loved her son deeply. Again she wondered why Nick despised her so.

Louisa's eyes glowed with a mother's love. What had this woman done?

When Jenny opened the door to her room later that evening, Nick stared, visibly shocked. Dressed in her new outfit, she was posed, confidant and very sophisticated, very polished. She'd declined the use of Louisa's jewelry, electing to wear her own pearl earrings and necklace.

Standing on the other side of the doorway, Jenny drank in the sight of her date, devastatingly handsome in a black tuxedo that complimented his dark hair and gray eyes. She was about to comment on how wonderful he looked and smelled, but his frown made her wary.

"That's quite a dress."

"I bought it on our little shopping trip today."

She twirled in a slow circle, giving him the full treatment. When she saw the male appreciation in his eyes, any lingering nerves she had about tonight disappeared.

"I had a great time today. Your mother treated me to lunch then we found this great little boutique. Like my purchase?"

"How could I not." His gaze warmed her from head to toe. "I know this really great jazz club in town. What do you say to ditching the party and taking off on our own?"

"Sounds like a great idea, but I don't think your father would understand. He really wants you there tonight."

"It was worth a shot. Maybe after the party."

She grinned. "Sounds good, but right now we should get going. I'm sure your folks don't want us to be late."

The party took place in the fashionable and well known Breakers Hotel, situated right by the ocean. Jenny knew it was a place to see and be seen. She gazed in awe at the Italian Renaissance style, the crystal chandeliers, and European furnishings. The twenty foot high windows facing the courtyard gardens and fountains intrigued her. What a place to study interior design, she marveled.

The group gathered in a private banquet room consisted of family and friends. Nick tucked her free hand in the crook of his arm as they began to circulate. The possessive touch filled her with a warmth she savored.

She clutched his arm as he led her around the room, introducing her to his father's friends and business associates. But she sensed the tension simmering beneath Nick's polite veneer. He clearly didn't want to be here.

Before they finished circling the room, Jenny had forgotten most of the names she heard. Everyone seemed pleased to meet her, especially Nick's childhood friends. She enjoyed the teasing and laughter at stories meant to embarrass him. His friends had a field day when a stunning brunette approached Nick, her sultry eyes fixed on her quarry. She sauntered right up to him, giving him a long, lusty kiss on the mouth.

"Why Nicky, I didn't know you were in town."

Nick stiffened, quickly moving away from the woman as his buddies chuckled. Displeasure radiated from him. Jenny pasted a calm smile on her face, her arm linked in his, showing solidarity. No matter who the other woman was, Nick had chosen Jenny to be here with him tonight. That was all that mattered.

"Ashley, it looks like you've got competition," one of the men in the group taunted.

Ah, so this was the woman in question.

Ashley glared down her perfect nose at Jenny, obviously not happy that Nick hadn't picked her to escort tonight. Being Nick's date held more surprises than Jenny had anticipated. And right about now she was growing tired of feeling like she just crawled out from under a rock. She squared her shoulders and gripped Nick's arm tighter.

"I thought you were coming alone," Ashley nearly purred in Nick's ear.

"I don't know why you'd think that." He pulled Jenny closer. "Besides, I don't go anywhere without Jenny."

Ashley's face turned red at the insinuation behind Nick's words. He didn't want her with him. With a pout, she turned and rushed away, hoots of laughter following in her wake. Jenny watched her go, trying to feel pity for the woman. But after the liberties she'd taken by kissing Nick, she decided that maybe Ashley deserved a little comeuppance.

"An old flame?" Jenny asked, gazing up at him.

"There's only been you," he answered, humor softening his dark expression.

"Pleased to hear it." She squeezed his arm, relieved that the tension from earlier had dissipated.

When Jenny finally got the chance, she steered Nick

toward Louisa and Charles, needing the connection to familiar faces. His father drew Nick into conversation, his lined face flushed with being the center of his son's attention. Louisa stood by her husband's side with a smile painted on her face that didn't reach her eyes. She seemed only sincerely happy when she watched Nick.

Across the room came rumblings of a commotion, then the crowd parted as Valerie and Howard came sweeping into their circle. Jenny smothered her annoyance as she watched the flamboyant woman make her entrance. She clearly resembled her father in looks and presence.

"Daddy, this is such a wonderful turnout," she gushed as she took hold of his arm. "I'm so proud of you!"

"Yes, sir," Howard chimed in. "So am I."

Nick punched his father's arm playfully. "Me, too. I'm glad you're getting the recognition for all the work you do, you deserve it."

Charles colored, then glanced at Louisa and wrapped his arm around her shoulders. His face softened as he looked down at her. "Actually, your mother did a lot of the work."

"Oh Daddy, please. You know that you're always the one involved in so many groups. For as long as I can remember you've hardly been home, with all the committees and boards you chair. You do all the meaningful work, not her."

"Well maybe that's about to change. I've been thinking—" Before he could finish, another well-wisher approached to shake his hand and pull him away from the family. Nick escaped to get refills for their glasses, leaving just the four.

"You know, Valerie," Howard said, a tick in his cheek quivering. "Your mother really does much of the work for your father. I've seen her in action, she's a real dynamo."

As Jenny glanced at the shallow woman, a guest bumped into her and she stumbled. Regaining her balance with the help of the apologizing man, she joined the group to catch the end of Valerie's cold remarks.

"Well I'm sure she's just sucking up to Daddy. God knows she needs to make up to him somehow." Her venomous gaze pierced Louisa's. "Are you having a good time, Mother? Probably not, there aren't any cowboys here to catch your fancy. If you like, Howard and I could drop you off at a country bar later so you don't have to inconvenience a taxi driver."

Finished with her diatribe, Valerie spun on her heel and gracefully sashayed across the room, all smiles. Howard followed with a frown on his face, clearly troubled by the words his wife had spoken in pure malice.

The revelation hit Jenny like a lightning bolt. Now she understood Nick's anger. Louisa had had an affair. That would explain the family tension.

Now, Nick's fear of commitment made sense, as well as the disdain he felt for his mother. It explained why he shied away from personal questions. His actions pointed toward hurt and betrayal, yet she'd missed the warning signs. Not having had experience with this type of family problem, she couldn't have realized the depth of Nick's feelings. But now she did. And it made her sad, for Nick and his mother.

With caution, she glanced at Louisa. The dread in the woman's eyes showed that she understood Jenny's revelation. Jenny started to speak, reached out her hand, but Louisa shook her head. Tears burned as she glimpsed the older woman's pain.

Louisa turned abruptly, fleeing from the glittering room. Jenny started to follow just as Nick returned.

"Where's the fire?" he asked, handing her a fresh drink.

"Please excuse me for a minute. I promise I'll be right back."

She had to keep from running to the door, wanting to appear decorous. They didn't need another scene.

As she entered the hallway, she caught sight of Louisa exiting the building. She took off in that direction and soon found herself in the gardens. Louisa sat on a marble bench, staring forlornly at the foliage.

Stepping up quietly, Jenny asked, "Do you mind if I join you?"

"No, please sit down." Tears choked Louisa's voice. She dabbed her eyes with a lace hanky, motioning for Jenny to join her on the bench. "I'm sorry you had to overhear that conversation. I'm afraid Valerie doesn't mind airing our dirty laundry in public, even though she doesn't always know what she's talking about."

Jenny bit her lip at the misery in Louisa's voice. "I honestly didn't know why Nick and Valerie were so openly hostile to you, but now that I've figured out the reason, I can't believe that your daughter would speak that way to you."

"I'm used to it," came the bitter reply. "The sad part is, everyone thinks I had an affair, but I didn't."

At Jenny's stunned expression, Louisa continued. "You said earlier that Nick didn't air our family secrets. Probably because he doesn't know the truth."

They fell silent for a moment. The occasional laughter and muffled music from somewhere in the building seemed an inappropriate backdrop to the continuing drama.

Jenny shivered. "Is there anything I can do?"

"Not unless you can convince Nick that I love him dearly." She sighed, the wrinkles around her eyes signaling her fatigue. "The sad part about the situation is that the children are angry with me, but Charles and I have come to an understanding. Unfortunately for them, the children were older during the worst part of our stormy relationship and it has affected each one deeply."

Jenny took Louisa's trembling hand in her own. "Have you ever tried to sit down with Nick and explain?"

Louisa shook her head. "I tried once when he was in college, but he wouldn't listen. He was so sure of himself then, so sure that I was wrong without exception.

"With only the two of us home alone now, Charles has come to realize that his never supporting me, always letting people believe the rumors, made things worse. But Nick hasn't been around to see the changes." A sad smiled curved her lips. "His father would never say a word to him, his pride gets in the way. So the only way he'll know what Charles and I have now is for me to tell him. I have to find a way to make him listen to me or else he'll always harbor anger. It's not good for him." Louisa fixed a solemn gaze on her. "Or for you."

Jenny agreed with that. How on earth did she begin to deal with this? Knowing Nick's reasons for being leery of commitment and helping him overcome that fear where two vastly different things. Unless he could see that the problem he so dreaded wasn't true.

Louisa took a shaky breath and squeezed Jenny's hand. "Let's go back inside before the men miss us. I don't want to have to explain our absence."

Jenny followed Louisa back into the building. As soon as she crossed the threshold into the room, Nick strode up to her. His eyes narrowed with concern. "Are you all right?"

"Yes," she said and grasped his warm hand with her own. They both watched his parents meet off to the side of the room, away from the guests.

"Is she okay?"

Jenny barely hid her astonishment at his question. "Do you want the truth, Nick?"

He looked at her, his face grim. "Yes. I want the truth."

She nodded. "The answer is no, she's not okay."

Nick stared at his parents, the facial mask falling into

place. Jenny recognized the defense maneuver for what it was, fear. If he locked out his emotions, nothing could touch or hurt him. She longed to comfort him, but he snapped out of his inner thoughts, leading her to a group of his friends.

For the remainder of the night, Nick continued to visit, but never asked Jenny what had happened to make his mother upset. She tried to understand, wondered how she would feel if her parents had this kind of problem. He'd buried the hurt that was surrounded by anger and she knew one day it would erupt.

She hoped he wouldn't regret the outcome.

Chapter Twelve

Jenny woke the following morning feeling out of sorts. She cracked her lids open to find that the room seemed unusually dark. The clock read eight o'clock. She wondered where the sun was.

She rose from the bed, her feet dragging along the carpet as she crossed the room to the window. Drawing the drapes aside, she glimpsed an overcast sky filled with heavy rain clouds lumbering by. The rain hadn't started yet, but having lived in Florida all of her life, she knew that with the skies growing darker, it was only a matter of time.

Changing quickly into jeans and a T-shirt, she thought about Nick, anxious to find him and see if his mood had improved from last night.

On impulse, she grabbed the small colorful basket she'd made for Louisa before they came to visit. She hurried to the dinning room, the rich aroma of coffee greeting her. In her haste to see Nick, she tripped on the edge of the carpet and stumbled into the room, nearly dropping her gift.

Nick lowered the newspaper he was reading and raised an eyebrow at her hasty appearance. Then he flashed her a quick smile. It didn't do much to calm her nerves, but at least he made an effort to act normal. She knew he was hurt, but she also knew the good side of him, despite his troubles. She'd have to keep remembering that.

Realizing that Louisa and Charles had also witnessed to her clumsy rush into the room, Jenny's face grew warm. She stood straight, calmly taking a seat and helping herself to coffee from the carafe placed at the center of the table. "Good morning, everyone."

"Have some breakfast," Louisa invited.

Charles lowered his paper enough to nod in greeting, then continued reading. Jenny sneaked a glance at Nick, only to find him staring at her with an unreadable expression shuttering his eyes. When he glimpsed her basket, his lips curved into a sort of grin as he reached for a triangle of buttered toast.

Jenny took a breath and handed the basket to Louisa. "I made this for you as a thank-you for inviting us to visit."

"Why Jenny, it's lovely. You made it?"

"It's a hobby," Nick informed his mother. "She's really talented."

Jenny blushed at his praise. The small gift worked as a talisman to draw conversation. Even Charles joined in.

"You should think about starting a business. That looks like fine quality work."

"I'm not interested in selling them," she explained. "I enjoy making them as gifts."

Nick folded the paper and placed it beside his coffee cup. "She doesn't have time, Dad. Now that I have the Chandler Group as clients, we'll be busy. Chandler wants Jenny's firm to do the interior design."

Charles peered at Jenny, then back to Nick. "So you'll be working together?"

"On this project. I'm hoping she'll do work for me again in the future."

Jenny raised an eyebrow in surprise. She knew Chandler wanted her to handle the design for the model home, but Nick hadn't mentioned her working with him in the future. Interesting.

"What do you have planned for today?" Louisa asked as she poured herself another cup of coffee, just as skilled as Nick at changing the subject. That would explain where he got it from.

"I'd like to see the Flagler mansion and tour the grounds," Jenny told Louisa. "Unless the weather gets really bad."

Nick glanced out the window. "I don't see why we can't give it a try. If it storms, we'll come back here."

Jenny sipped her coffee, another idea forming in her mind. If Nick and his mother spent time together, maybe they'd be able to discuss their problems. Nick seemed approachable this morning, so he might not argue about another person joining their sightseeing expedition. If they were thrown together, they'd have to talk. She smiled, mentally patting herself on the back for her brainstorm.

"Louisa," Jenny asked, "would you like to join us?"

Louisa looked up from her plate, surprise evident in her gray eyes. She quickly glanced at Nick, just in time to see a deep line furrowing his forehead. She hesitated. "No, dear. You go on and be by yourselves. You don't need me tagging along."

So much for the major idea of the year. She wasn't very good at this meddling thing. This was more of a job for Kate.

With the flick of his wrist, Charles expertly closed and folded his newspaper in one fluid motion. "It was thoughtful of you to offer, but Louisa and I have been invited to a luncheon with friends. We'll be gone most of the afternoon."

He smiled at his wife, Jenny noticed, with a rare turn of his lips that seemed to be a genuine show of emotion. She hoped Nick saw the exchange, how the older couple acknowledged each other with a special look. Maybe then he would see that things do change.

"Come on," Nick said in an impatient tone as he rose from the chair. "Let's get going." He nodded brusquely to his parents, then, his shoulders stiff, he started to exit the room. But not before she glimpsed the surprise in his eyes. Had he seen his parents affectionate glances?

He took one last wide-eyed look at them before grabbing Jenny's hand to pull her along.

Oh yeah, he noticed.

During the ride to the museum, Nick remained silent, but Jenny couldn't resist asking the question on her mind.

"Did you notice how your father smiled at your mother? It's almost as if they're sharing a special secret."

"They are," Nick grumbled. "I'm surprised he wasn't glaring at her instead."

"Maybe they know something you don't."

"I don't want to know anything."

Jenny stifled a curt response. She knew he needed to come to grips with his parent's past so he could move on, but she couldn't force him to make any decisions. Frustration sliced bone deep. She hated feeling powerless to help him.

The Flagler mansion, Whitehall, sat majestically in the drab afternoon light. Flagler had built the impressive home for his third wife, and was responsible for developing much of the Palm Beach area.

Jenny smiled with excitement as they entered the venerable old house through the bronze double doors. She loved historical sights and the decorative arts, soaking up the atmosphere that would influence her designing ideas.

Inside the marble entrance, she gasped in delight. Not only was this house historical, it had an air of romance about it too. To think that a man would build something lasting for the woman he loved touched her heart. Would Nick be that kind of man? She knew she should head those thoughts in a different direction, but the more time she spent with Nick, the more she knew fighting her feelings for him was a losing battle.

They moved through the foyer and joined the next tour group. Jenny could almost feel herself transported into the past. She could imagine the laughter and joyous times all around her. This household had been happy, she could feel the contentment all around her.

Her whimsical thoughts were interrupted by the warm grasp of Nick's hand in hers. She leaned toward him, reveling in that lightheaded rush that accompanied a touch from him. If she lived to be one hundred, she knew there would always be this tingle of excitement when he stood nearby or when he gazed at her with those intense gray eyes.

They followed the tour and strolled through the house hand in hand, entering rooms decorated from a sixteenth century library to an Elizabethan breakfast room.

"Don't get any ideas," Nick whispered in a droll tone, his breath splaying along her exposed neck.

"Too late. I have all kinds of ideas," she teased. "But I promise not to go overboard decorating your model home." She focused on her surroundings again. "This place is huge. With your architectural expertise, how long do you think it took to build this place?"

"I'd say eighteen months."

"That's a pretty good guess."

He grinned. "Actually, I read it somewhere."

Jenny laughed out loud, earning a frown from the tour guide. She lowered her voice in the hushed surroundings. "I can't imagine living in a home this size. I'm so busy as it is, I'd never have time for housework."

"You could hire help, you know."

She placed her hand over her heart and spoke in a mock southern accent. "And let a stranger do all the work? Never. I'd have to clean before the maid arrived."

Nick chuckled. "If Chandler decides to hire you for more projects, you won't have time to clean."

She wagged a finger at him. "Never underestimate a woman and her home. Tidiness is a sacred bond we Meyer's cherish."

Laughing softly, Nick led her to another room. "I promise never to interfere with you and your domestic rules."

"Thank you."

They stepped into the next room, yet again another showplace. Jenny wandered to a window and peeked outside. The clouds still seemed ominous, the hibiscus plants and crepe myrtle swayed in the gusty wind. She shivered and wrapped her arms around her for warmth, silently berating herself for putting so much stock in foreboding images lately. Taking a deep breath, she continued with the tour.

Before leaving the grounds, they stopped to admire a private railway car parked on the grounds.

"What a way to travel," Nick remarked before a few fat raindrops splattered on their heads. He squinted into the sky. "Lovely Florida weather."

They sprinted to the Corvette for cover. Fog formed on the windows as their damp bodies gave off heat in the cool interior. Nick put his arm around her shoulder and tugged her to him. She placed a hand on his chest for balance and stared up at his face, delighting in the scent of his cologne. Raindrops hit the top of the car in a steady rhythm and the vehicle formed an intimate cocoon.

Nick's gaze held hers for a long moment until he lowered his head and brushed her lips with his. His free hand tilted her chin to give his mouth better access. She inched closer, the stick shift digging into her thigh, and bunched his shirt in her fist to draw him closer.

A clap of thunder jarred the intimacy. Nick lifted his head to glance out the window, then turned to her with a look of surprise. "What was I thinking? Kissing you in my car in broad daylight in a public parking lot."

"At least you're kissing me. After last night, I wasn't so sure."

"I'd rather we didn't go there."

Jenny fumed. "I wish you wouldn't always shut me out. Friends, remember?"

He stared out the rain dappled window.

"Or is that the problem? You don't want to be friends anymore."

Stunned, he turned toward her. "Why would you say that?"

"Look, I know we haven't had the most . . . traditional dating relationship, but I thought maybe you'd start to take me into your confidence, trust me a little."

"Of course I trust you. I never would have brought you here if I didn't."

They sat in static silence for long minutes. Jenny listened to the rain hitting the car roof and wondered what really went on in Nick's brain. It wasn't so much that she was getting mixed signals from him, he'd been up front about his fear of commitment. But still, he continued to see her exclusively and Jenny couldn't help but wonder where that would lead them.

Nick broke the silence. "Let's go get lunch."

Jenny controlled her mounting disappointment while Nick drove them to the restaurant, a local favorite. She had no idea how to get Nick to let his defenses down with her. Maybe they'd been better off with the dating lessons and no personal baggage.

Once inside, they were escorted to a table and as they settled in, she glanced around the old fashioned gambling casino that had been turned into a trendy restaurant. She focused her attention on Nick, who was staring across the room. "What's so interesting?"

"An old girlfriend."

"Really?" Jenny shifted to look over her shoulder. "Where is she?"

"The young blond woman sitting with the older man."

Jenny caught sight of the couple and turned back to

face Nick. "Her father?"

"Hardly."

Placing her elbows on the table, she leaned forward and rested her chin on folded hands. "Hmm. And this bothers you?"

"About as much as your ex and the boss's daughter."

Jenny stared at him. "Meaning?"

He shot her a smile that didn't reach his eyes. "She dumped me for a rich older guy when we were in college. It seems her taste in men has only . . . matured."

"Then we seem to have more in common that I thought." Jenny sipped water from the glass set in front of her. She didn't like this strange mood Nick had descended into and she planned to let him know, but he spoke first.

"There's more to it."

"What do you mean?"

"We were sort of engaged."

"Sort of?"

"Not officially. We talked about it, made a decision, but kept it quiet. With all the problems at home, I wanted to hold on to this private decision for a little while. We were going to make the announcement during the summer break."

Nick and his secrets. A shadow crossed over his face and Jenny dreaded hearing the next part. "Go on."

"She dropped out early and came home while I finished the semester. My sweet sister called to inform me that my girlfriend was playing around with an older, faster set, and an older, faster, guy. She didn't deny it when I confronted her, so I broke it off with her. I haven't seen her since, but I've heard stories."

"Why didn't you tell me this before?"

He shrugged. "I don't know. It was so long ago. It didn't really seem important."

"Any part of your life is important to me."

He glanced down into his drink, then back to her. "I suppose that's why I offered to help you the first time we met. I knew what it felt like to be disappointed."

"And here I thought it was my sparkling personality."

A small smile played at his lips.

No wonder he had such a hard time believing relationships could work. Every time she turned around there were new glimpses into Nick's past. And with each new revelation his emotional walls seemed to go up higher.

Maybe it was time to tell him that she loved him. That she'd never betray his confidences. That she understood his pain. He had to trust someone, it might as well be her.

"Nick—"

"I don't want to dwell on this."

She frowned. "Don't you think it's about time? You owe me the truth of your feelings, Nick. I brought all my skeletons out of the closet. I trusted you. But you seem to be slipping deeper and deeper into the past and closing me off."

With a sigh, he ran his hand through his wind-blown hair, then reached for his glass of water.

He's procrastinating, she thought glumly. He's going to tell me something I don't want to hear.

"Every time I come home, I find myself despising the lifestyle I grew up in. The way my parents tolerated each other for years. I go back to Clearwater and find myself again, but I can't get the feel of this place out of my bones." He pierced her with his aching gaze. "My family doesn't make it easy and I know you mean well, but trying to bring my mother and me together makes everything harder."

Jenny blushed, embarrassed by her transparent scheme to unite mother and son. She tried to explain, but Nick waved a hand to quiet her.

"You want the truth and nothing but? Okay, here goes. I'm afraid I'll hurt you, Jenny, like others have hurt me. That maybe the ability to tear apart another person's heart is genetic. It doesn't make sense, but it's a fear I've lived with for years. My mother and I are very much alike. If she could make a mistake, then I could too."

"Nick, what ever happened is between your parents, not you. Yes, you suffer the results, but what if they've come to terms with their mistakes? If you really want our relationship to work, you have to see that. Otherwise we don't have a chance."

Melancholy shadowed the gray in his eyes, turning them darker. "I instinctively trusted you from the start. I knew you wouldn't hurt me on purpose and I grabbed onto that like a lifeline, wanting it to last forever. That's why I agreed to the lessons. I thought you, or us together, could save me from these unwanted feelings I have. But the doubts keep pressing until I can't see a way out."

"You're right, I won't hurt you. But you have to give a little too. Maybe you can start by talking to your parents. Find out what they think, how they've dealt with the past. Then maybe we will have a chance at long lasting happiness." She paused and took a deep breath. "I love you, Nick. I have since the day you gave me that special shell as a gift. You are the most remarkable thing in my life."

Nick closed his eyes and Jenny wondered where he went with his thoughts. But when he looked at her again, the same despair crystallized and she realized he still couldn't let go of the past. Nor could he say the words she wanted to hear. "Let's go," she suggested, not in the mood for lunch or continuing this conversation.

As Nick unlocked the passenger door, she gave him an ultimatum. "You have to decide, Nick. The past or me."

They drove back to the house in tense silence. The house was deathly quiet. Jenny's emotions were too raw to start up the conversation, so when they entered Nick's bedroom, she sat on the bed and stared out the window. The afternoon sky grew more cloudy and a gloom settled over the room.

Nick sat at his desk, fiddling with an odd shaped paperweight. He laughed suddenly, a mirthless sound that reached out and squeezed Jenny's heart. She looked over at him, silently questioning his outburst.

"I have a woman in my bedroom, my parents aren't

home, and after the fool I made of myself at the restaurant, I can't even take advantage of the situation."

Jenny smiled through tears that blurred her vision. She swiped at her eyes and rose from the bed to cross the room. "I'll be right back."

She hurried to her room, rummaging through the bags she'd gathered from her shopping spree the day before. Fishing out a small bag, she returned to Nick's room. With an uneasy smile, she handed him his gift.

He looked from the bag up to her. "What's this?"

"A memento," she answered, her heart slamming into her chest.

Reaching into the bag, he withdrew a carved figure. He stared at it for what seemed an eternity. "How did you know about my collection?"

"Your mother took me to the memorabilia store yesterday. She told me all about your hobby, so I wanted to give you an addition. I hope you like it."

Sighing, Nick clasped the soldier in his palm, then slowly rose from the chair. He paused to stare into her eyes, his stormy gaze caressing every part of her face. They stayed locked for seconds until he moved to the closet.

Opening the door, he reached up to the top shelf, his muscles molded against his cotton shirt as he grabbed hold of a large metal box. He carried it to the bed and gingerly laid it on the spread. "This is it."

He lifted the lid and Jenny peered inside, curious to view the contents. They sat on either side of the case, pulling out different figurines as Nick explained each one. In an odd way, she'd never felt closer to him. Today he'd been totally honest with her and shared a part of himself he'd kept hidden for so long. He may not have said he loved her, but she knew his feelings for her ran deep.

In silence she watched his expression range from delight at his old possessions, to melancholy at the way his life had developed. He wasn't a knight in shining armor come to slay life's disappointments and she loved him more at this moment than she thought possible.

As he took another figure from the box, she reached out her hand to his and held on tightly. He grew tense, but she raised his hand to her lips and gently kissed his clenched fist. He made a soft sound, of pain or pleasure, she didn't know. All she wanted was to bask in her love for him and try to take his pain away.

He pulled back and Jenny saw a glimmer of gentleness in his eyes.

"Where are you going?"

"I'll be out in the living room. I . . ." He stopped speaking and opened the door. He glanced at her one final time, then left the room.

Nick leaned against the wall after closing the door to his bedroom. He took several cleansing breaths. Now, more than ever, confusion held him in a strangle hold. A deep ache burned in his heart. Love? Could it be? He'd never felt it before. Somehow Jenny had managed to slip under his defenses. It had been gradual, but she'd done it nonetheless. And it scared him. What if he let her down? What if he lost her unwavering commitment, her love and respect?

He'd admitted a lot to Jenny today, more than he'd shared with anyone in his life. As much as he wanted to cling to her, to the inner strength she possessed, he couldn't. It felt like his fingers were slipping on a greased rope. Like the life preserver kept bobbing out of reach. He hated the feeling, but continued to feel powerless to stop it.

Voices at the other end of the house distracted him from his miserable thoughts. His parents. Maybe Jenny was right. Maybe he had to face the past to hold on to the future.

Chapter Thirteen

A short while later, Jenny entered the living room to find Nick with his mother. She stopped short, not wanting to disturb them. Taking a step back, she halted when Nick called her name, worried about the anger she heard there.

"Jenny, wait."

Jenny stepped into the living room with trepidation. The tension level here was sky high. "I think I should go back to my room."

"No, stay for the fireworks. You're the one who wanted me to get this all out in the open."

Jenny cringed at his words. She glanced over at Louisa who stood at the far end of the room, her hands clasped in a tight knot.

"You wanted to know what this woman had done to me."

"She didn't do anything to you," Jenny corrected. "In fact, she didn't do anything at all. Maybe you should blame your father, instead."

Nick's brows angled down in puzzlement. "What makes you say that? Just when did you find out about our family secrets?"

"Last night."

"I see." He looked at his mother, his voice tempered anger as he spoke. "Did you cry on her sympathetic shoulder?"

"No—" Louisa started to explain before Jenny interrupted.

"Nick, if you would listen to your mother, you'd find that what happened isn't what you think. The memories of your parent's arguing have been blown out of proportion."

"Since when did you become an expert on domestic family problems? Your family has as many problems as Ozzie and Harriet. Getting you married off seems to be the highlight of their life."

Jenny's face grew warm. "That's uncalled for, Nick."

He had the grace to look sorry for his words. "I'm sorry. You took me by surprise."

"Perhaps we should all calm down before we say things we shouldn't," Louisa suggested.

"Maybe you should have thought of that when you decided to mess up this family's lives. Or haven't you noticed that your children are incapable of having normal relationships with their spouses? What number divorce is Susan on? Thanks a lot Mother, we all appreciate it."

He glared at her and a fissure of fear unsettled Jenny as he regarded her like the enemy for defending his mother. Maybe in his thinking he considered her a traitor, but she never meant to betray him.

Nick's words echoed in her mind. *I instinctively trusted you.*

Panic suddenly closed off her throat. She wanted to explain, but the words wouldn't come.

"I'm going out," Nick announced. He strode across the room, his desire to leave evident in every angry step he took.

"Wait, Nick," Jenny called as her reached the foyer. "Where are you going?"

"I don't know. Out. Away from here."

"Just like that? Don't you think you should stay and resolve the problem?"

"I don't feel like talking. Why don't you do it for me since you seem to have all the answers."

She reached out to catch his arm, but he pulled out of reach. "I'm sorry," she whispered, fear knotting her stomach.

"Of all the people in the world that I expected to be honest with me, you were the only one I could depend on. You finally figured out what our family problem is and you didn't tell me. Didn't you think I'd want to know when you discovered the truth?"

She had to make him understand. "Nick, I wasn't sure what to do. You didn't want to talk last night and I didn't want to tell you in a restaurant. It was quite by accident that I found out. It's not like I intentionally went snooping around and then kept the knowledge of what I found from you. I wish you would sit down and listen to your mother. She has something important to tell you."

The lines around his eyes deepened and his shoulders slumped in resignation. He lightly touched her cheek with his hand, then left the house.

"It's going to storm," Jenny whispered, reaching out to place her hand on the cold door. Louisa came up behind her, placing comforting hands on her shoulders. They stood silently for a few moments until a clap of thunder brought Jenny back to her senses.

She jerked open the door and ran onto the porch. Black clouds hung overhead and cold raindrops began to fall. She ran down the steps to Nick's car and peered inside to find the interior empty. Moisture ran into her eyes as she turned to Louisa who stood on the porch, her arms crossed over her chest.

Jenny looked over the grounds but didn't see Nick. "He didn't take the car. He'll get drenched."

"Come back inside, dear. He'll be back when he's ready."

Reluctantly, Jenny dragged her feet up the steps and onto the porch. "Maybe if he walks off some steam he'll be easier to deal with."

Louisa glanced out at the steady rain and frowned. "If he's anything like his father, he'll just bury it deeper, believing the problem can't touch him then. It doesn't work, as Charles found out. It only makes things worse."

"Maybe both of you can talk to him. You said Charles doesn't like to discuss problems, but if he realizes that his son's well-being is at stake here, he might reconsider."

Louisa put her arm around Jenny's shoulder and led her into the house. "It might just work," she agreed.

The two women who loved Nick more than anything in the world waited patiently for him to return. The wind blew stronger and the rain fell more heavily. The afternoon turned to twilight and the sky grew darker, casting a pall over the living room. Jenny shivered until Louisa draped a cotton blanket over her. They drank coffee, each lost in her own thoughts. It had grown totally black outside when Charles found them still seated in the living room, no lights on.

"Why the devil are you sitting in the dark?"

"Charles, we need to talk," Louisa said firmly.

He switched a light on, his forehead creasing with worry. "What's wrong?"

"It's Nick."

The older man sighed. "I thought so."

Louisa's eyes widened in surprise. "I didn't think you noticed. You never said a word."

"I know my son and I can see that he's been troubled for quite some time."

"Why haven't you said anything?" Jenny asked, angry that this man saw his son in pain and chose to ignore it.

Charles frowned, running his hand through graying

hair. Jenny's heart ached at the gesture she found so endearing in Nick being imitated by his father.

"There have been many times when I wanted to approach him, Jenny, but something always held me back. Pride, fear . . . I'm not sure anymore."

"I told Jenny," Louisa said as Charles joined her on the sofa. "I told her that everyone thought I'd had an affair, but it wasn't true. I didn't tell her your part of it."

Charles sighed. "It was a long time ago and I finally reached a point in my life where I accept the truth, and the truth is that I pushed Louisa away. She cried on the shoulder of an old friend, but she never betrayed me. I acted as if she did by ignoring her and putting business first. My actions made everyone believe the worst of her.

"As you get older, your priorities change. One day I saw what my marriage had become, how my children had suffered. Unfortunately, I never bothered to let my children in on that truth. They believed the worst and I let them, all because of my pride. I'm as much to blame, if not more, for the way they view their mother."

Jenny tugged the blanket closer, fighting to keep her shattered nerves composed for a few minutes longer. "Please tell Nick what you just told me. You're his father. He'll listen to you."

She stood, the blanket falling unheeded from her trembling shoulders to the sofa. "I pray he's not blinded by pride, Mr. Bryson. If he is, then I'll lose him for sure and I couldn't bear that." Tears flooded from her eyes as she pleaded, her voice husky with emotion. "Please talk to him."

Louisa took her husband's hand in her own. Finally, he nodded. Jenny left them alone to talk while she went to her room to wait.

Nick returned home before midnight, soaked, heading straight to his bathroom. He shed his damp clothes before standing under the scalding shower for a long time. Now that he was home, what would he do? His walk had proved fruitless, the anger and disappointment swirling in him just a fresh as earlier in the day. It felt like a punch to his gut when Jenny had sided with his mother. How would he get over that? He still had no answers when he walked back into the bedroom fifteen minutes later to drag on dry clothes.

As much as he dreaded it, he knew he had to talk to Jenny. He knew she'd be worried about him, but he couldn't help it. He'd needed to walk, needed time alone.

He knocked lightly on Jenny's door. When she didn't answer, he cracked the door open a bit to peer inside. Jenny lay on the bed under a blanket, her eyes bright as she stared at him.

"Are you okay?" she whispered.

"I'm not sure," he answered, then stepped just inside the room.

Jenny sat up and turned on the light. He got a glimpse of her red-rimmed eyes, her mussed hair and a tinge of guilt ran through him. Maybe he shouldn't have left her alone.

"Have you spoken to your parents yet?" she asked.

He frowned. "No. They're still up?"

"Yes. They have something to tell you."

"Maybe I don't want to hear what they have to say," he answered, hating to admit he was curious.

"Please," she said, her voice raw.

"For a few minutes." He turned to walk from the room, but stopped, looking over his shoulder at her. "I know you wanted to help, Jenny. I've never had anyone in my life that cared so much about me. I should have appreciated that, not gotten angry with you."

A smile trembled on her lips. "Then go talk to your parents. They love you too."

Nick nodded, swallowing past the lump in his throat. All day long he wondered why Jenny put up with him. Because she loved him? Maybe there was more to life than fighting the past. He knew if he wanted a chance with Jenny, he'd have to let go.

He headed down the hallway, finding his mother, alone, in the living room. She sat in the couch staring into space, her face drawn and tired. He coughed and she jerked, then looked at him. An inviting smile curved her lips and she beckoned him to sit beside her by patting the cushion with her hand. With weary resignation, he joined her, careful not to sit close enough to touch.

"You made it home, I see."

"Yes."

"Are you ready for the truth now?"

Nick stared into her eyes, so much like his own, afraid to know what the truth really was. He nodded, unable to voice any of his hidden fears.

"I was in love with another man when my father decided I should marry Charles. Your father was quite a catch, the only son of a prosperous family, already active in the family business. Also very popular and very attractive." She brushed back a wisp of hair, then folded her hands in her lap.

"I had my own ideas about my future. The man I loved was a ranch hand with no college education or generations of wealthy relatives. He was honest and hardworking, the most wonderful man I had ever met."

She smiled as though lost in the memory of happier times. Nick shifted, uncomfortable with the confession.

"We planned to marry. We spent hours talking about the future, how we wanted children and someday our own ranch. He was smart and I had faith that all our dreams would come true. I never thought for one minute those dreams would shatter."

She paused, taking a deep breath. Heartache crept into her soft voice. "My father found out about the relationship on the night he announced that the Bryson family was coming to visit. I knew what that meant. That Charles was the man he had selected for my husband. I told Daddy my plans and he was furious. He swore he would disown me if I didn't do what he commanded."

Louisa stopped again to catch her breath. Her eyes

had a sheen of moisture over them, her drawl more pro-
nounced in her distress. "You have to remember Nick,
when I was young you did as your parents instructed,
even if you hated the idea. In despair, I gave in and married your father. Together we united two prestigious
families.

"When I think back on it, I realize I never had the
strength to defy my father. I had been brought up with
everything and anything at my disposal. If I had followed my heart, I would have been denied material
things, but I would have had love. My father convinced
me that love alone would never be enough."

She smiled a melancholy grin. "I grew to like your
father, and at first we had a good marriage. When he
became more busy with work, I had you children to
raise and eventually we grew apart. By this time you
were older and noticed the distance and indifference."

"So when did you cheat on him?" Nick asked defiantly, cruelly.

"That's the ironic thing. I never did." Louisa brushed
at her immaculate skirt, a nervous habit he had seen for
years. Her voice grew husky as she answered. "Do you
recall the time I went to take care of your grandmother
when she was gravely ill? I saw my old boyfriend. We
were surprised to see each other at first. He still harbored
a deep resentment at me for leaving, although with time
he came to understand. After a tentative meeting, I discovered that the childhood love I had for him was a
memory. I knew I loved Charles. Had for years. But your
father heard I had seen him and thought the worst."

Nick stood, crossing the room to stare out into the pitch black night. He didn't want his mother's story to touch him, despite remembering all the nights she stayed home alone, waiting for his father. There were many nights when Nick waited with her.

"Eventually, your father came to believe me. And was sorry he'd thought the worst of me."

"That's the truth," a gruff voice interrupted.

Nick whirled around to see his father silhouetted in the doorway. "I did push your mother away, Nick. I knew she didn't love me when we got married, so I thought staying away from her would salvage my pride. It only succeeded in making a much larger problem for everyone. I never trusted her, son, and it's the biggest mistake I ever made."

Nick looked from his father to mother as they stood side by side, a united front. He pushed his hands into his pants pockets, letting his head fall back as he stared at the ceiling.

"I know you've been hurt by all this, Nick," Louisa said. "Your father and I should have been more honest with you so that you could trust your ability to be involved in a loving relationship. We can't change the past, I can only encourage you with the future. Charles and I finally looked at each other and realized that the love was there, we just had to work at sharing it. And we have.

"You have a special friend in Jenny and it's obvious that she loves you. Many marriages do work, Nick, and if you are lucky enough to find the right person to share your life with, hold on with all your strength."

Nick expelled his pent-up breath. "How can I trust someone when my own family has never had trust amongst themselves? How can I suddenly forget all the lies, the hypocrisy I've seen in your marriage and expect it can be any better for me?"

"I guess you take that risk," Charles advised. "I don't think you would have brought Jenny here if you didn't have feelings for her, especially in the light of this family's history. You trusted her, son, but don't make her pay for our mistakes."

Nick nodded, his father's words echoing hollow in his ears. They'd finally been honest with him, but the damage was already done.

He crossed the room, pausing before Louisa. He bent down to place a goodnight kiss on her forehead, something he hadn't done in years, then he shook his father's hand.

The dark bedroom was quiet when Nick went back to Jenny's room. She was sound asleep on the bed, propped against the pillows. The hall light streamed into the room, touching her face.

A loud clap of thunder disturbed her and she moaned softly, rolling over. Nick pulled the spread around her shoulders. He stood silently, watching her breathe steadily in her slumber. Another round of thunder jolted him from his deep thoughts. He turned and left the room, soundlessly closing the door behind him.

Chapter Fourteen

Jenny joined the family the next morning, stopping short when she saw their serious faces viewing the television. "The storm has intensified through the night," the weatherman forecasted grimly. "The worst of the storm has left the immediate Palm Beach area, but continues to move across the state, picking up momentum to unleash its fury on the west coast of Florida. Especially hard hit are the coastal and surrounding areas of Pinellas County. A tornado touched down in Clearwater, with record winds and heavy rain. Many residential areas were damaged as a result, with homes destroyed and tree debris cluttering the roads. Residents in low lying areas are urged to evacuate or remain inside in higher elevations, keeping the roadways free. Emergency vehicles are out in full force and local authorities want as little traffic as possible until the weather improves."

Stepping into the breakfast nook, Jenny watched the television screen as it transmitted scenes of the storm's destruction as it whipped over land and sea. Waves smashed boat docks. Driving winds uprooted trees and tore shingles from roofs. As the camera panned in on one specific neighborhood, Jenny gasped a she recognized the homes in the vicinity of the house Nick was building. She glanced at him, seeing the grave concern etched into his features as the report continued.

Outside the winds had died down, but the skies remained overcast. No one had realized how strong this storm would be as it picked up strength on its journey across the peninsula, least of all Jenny, who had weathered a different storm of her own.

"I think we should go home," Nick said, his gaze still glued to the news report.

"Oh, Nick," Louisa implored. "You can't go into that weather."

"She's right, son. At least wait a few hours until the worst has passed, then start making your way home."

Jenny excused herself from the breakfast table, her mind replaying the images she'd just seen. Thinking about her family in the midst of the violent storm, her heart beat wildly. When she got back to the bedroom, she called her parents from the bedroom phone, thankful to hear that they were all safe.

Nick found her a few minutes later. She folded her

clothes as calmly as possible to place in the open suit-case. "What are you doing?"

She forced a grin. "I know you well enough to real-ize you won't wait for the storm to subside before we head home. I'm getting ready to leave." She folded a shirt, absently pressing out the wrinkles. "Do you think your house was destroyed?"

Nick raked his fingers through his hair. "I hope not, but things look pretty bad there."

"I'll keep my fingers crossed," she promised.

He started to say something, then shook his head as he moved to the window. She watched his wooden movements, almost afraid to uncover the reason. The tension at the breakfast table seemed to stem from the weather report, not the personal onslaught the family had faced. Needing to find out, she took a deep breath and asked.

"How did the conversation with your parents go last night?"

If it was at all possible, he grew even more rigid. "The truth came out, if that's what you mean."

She sat on the edge of the bed. "And?"

He glanced at her. "And what?"

"How did you respond?"

"I listened. I saw they were being truthful. Then I went to bed."

She gritted her teeth. "All so calm and composed?"

"What did you want me to do? Scream and yell? Throw things around?"

"No, of course not. I just thought you'd have more of a reaction."

"Look, it's their problem. If they can deal with it, so can I."

But can you really, Jenny wondered with a sinking sensation in her stomach.

Within the hour, after much concerned debate from his parents, Nick and Jenny were in the car heading home. He kept the radio tuned into the weather updates, hoping for good news, but the forecasters proclaimed the storm as a major catastrophe, almost as devastating as a hurricane.

In the hours it took to drive to Tampa, the news reported that the heavy precipitation had moved out over the Gulf, losing intensity. Light drizzle misted against the windshield and the winds had gentled. By the time they reached Clearwater, Nick's stomach knotted with apprehension. The skies were a leaden gray and the clouds continued to roll swiftly by.

He drove cautiously, even though emergency crews had cleaned up many of the streets. However, the result of the storms effects could be seen everywhere; upturned trees, mobile homes leaning at crazy angles, broken windows.

Instead of dropping Jenny off first, Nick headed for the lot of his house. The one he intended to make his home. He had to know if the structure had withheld the storm. In his mind, if the house stood, so would their relationship. If the house survived the storm, they could stand against anything. He knew he was reaching, that his analogy was flawed, but he had to know.

He approached the lot slowly, as if he already knew what to expect. His heart sank when he saw the damage to the partially constructed house. The trusses toppled like dominos, smashed apart on the cement foundation by the intensity of the storm. The walls had caved in, windows blown out, the front door knocked down and hanging crookedly on its hinges. Two by fours lay strewn across the property, scattered haphazardly by the winds. Large bundles of shingles, once neatly wrapped, were ripped open and dumped onto the cement block and the muck in front of the house.

"Stay in the car," he told Jenny. "I don't want you to get hurt."

Numb with shock at the devastation, Nick opened the car door, leaning against it as he stood to survey the damage. His hands shook as he slammed the door and slowly walked through the devastation that had been the beginning of his house. He mindlessly kicked at stray lumber as he crossed the front yard. At one spot his feet sank into a mud puddle. He pulled himself free, only to lose his balance and stumble. He caught himself before hitting the ground. Finally he made it to the building and stood at the threshold, his hands clenched around the sides of the door as he jerked it free, anger infusing his desperation to straighten the door.

He heard Jenny come up from behind him. "Nick, it'll be all right."

He dropped the heavy piece and swung around, lashing out at her, frustration making his words sharp. "Please go back to the car. It's not safe wandering around all this damage."

She ignored him further by coming to stand beside him. "You can rebuild, Nick. The lumber will have to be replaced, but the foundation is solid. With a little hard work, you'll have this place repaired in no time. I'll even help you."

"It's more than a house, Jenny," he said with a sigh. "It was a dream. My dream. This whole weekend has been a nightmare. First my parents, now this. My life is crumbling around me, just like the remains of this house. I don't know if I can pick any of this up and start again."

"Of course you can." Jenny pointed to the clutter around them. "These are just things, Nick. They can be replaced, rebuilt."

"They can, but I don't know if I can," he said in a hoarse whisper. He turned to face her, trying to bury the guilt when he glimpsed her startled face. He knew he was going to hurt her, despite all his good intentions and high ideals. And it was pretty clear that she knew it too.

He took her arm and guided her back to the car, being careful to keep her from tripping over the wreckage. Once safely inside the car, he drove straight to Jenny's apartment.

The complex was untouched, a stark reminder of the erratic patterns of the storm's destructive path. Inside, her apartment was as tidy as ever. He stayed by the door, his heart beating so hard he was sure she could hear it in the quiet room. He doubted he could have moved if a tornado chose that moment to rip through the apartment.

She looked at him, eyes wide, hands at her sides, her silence daring him to say something. Anything.

He obliged.

"I thought I could handle everything that's happened, but I was wrong. So much has happened in a few short days. I have a lot of sorting out to do before I can ever be more to you than a friend."

"I meant it when I said I loved you."

"I know that." A twinge of guilt raced through him when she winced at his answer. He wanted to return the words, felt them in his heart, but fear made him close up.

Her face paled. "I thought you had enough trust in me to take a chance, that you would see that some people can make a promise and keep their word."

"I did trust you. Do trust you." The room suddenly shrunk and turned warm. He pulled at his collar, but the heat of Jenny's gaze made him more uncomfortable.

Couldn't she see his dilemma? Couldn't she realize how fearful he was of making the mistake his parents had? He wouldn't put her through that. "I've fought commitment for so long, I'd almost forgotten what I was running from. Then you came along, innocent and trusting. I even forgot I was afraid of marriage, or at least I was coming to terms with the idea. I started to believe in the fantasy of a home and family." He slumped against the wall, the energy slowly draining from him. "But this weekend opened up all the doors of uncertainty that you had slammed shut. I looked at my parents and realized I wasn't much better than they were." She tried to cut in, but he held up a hand and pushed himself straight, shaking his head. "You deserve better, Jenny."

Jenny crossed her arms over her chest, her face a rigid mask of hurt. "Don't I have a say in the matter?"

He shoved his hands into his pockets, trying to ignore the pain in his chest, the terror that she would be as confused and hurt as he was. This alone made him act on pure fear. "I'm ending this before you hate me."

"I could never hate you, but I do disagree with your decision," she told him sharply.

He grimaced at her words.

"You can't hide any longer. That's what you've been doing all these years. I finally figured it out. If you blame your parents, then you don't have to own up to the fact that *Nick* is afraid of trusting. You trusted your mother, she let you down. You trusted an old girlfriend and she also let you down. So now you're afraid to let anyone else close, afraid they'll eventually let you down. It's easier to hide than face the facts, isn't it Nick? It's easier not to love, then no one expects anything from you and you won't be disappointed. You hide, no one touches you. Well, I love you. With no hidden agenda. I'm sorry you think you could never love me, because you're wrong."

Nick stared at a point above her shoulder, unable to make eye contact. If he did, it would be like a punch to his solar plexus. He wouldn't be able to breathe. She was right about his inability to commit, but she was wrong that he didn't love her. He just didn't have to courage to tell her so.

She took a tentative step closer. "When I met you, you made a point of being spontaneous, out for fun all the time. No serious entanglements. That's just another symptom of the hurt. Keeping everyone at bay. Except me.

"But now you want to leave, with another excuse. I know you hurt Nick, but if you walk out that door, you'll hurt me as badly as you've been hurt."

"That's what I've been afraid of all along," he said with resignation. He'd already made up his mind. "You need a guy who can sort out his past from his future. I can't do that right now."

He took the keys from his pocket, ready to bolt from the apartment. She stubbornly stood her ground, refusing to take part in his desertion. When he realized she was waiting for him to make the last move, he stared at her for one last, long minute, before he spoke heavily. "I'm sorry."

Then he was gone.

Jenny stared at the door in disbelief as it closed behind him.

Solid. Definite. Final.

Just like the determined expression in Nick's eyes before he left. He'd made his decision and it didn't include her. She felt foolish and numb.

Very numb.

She turned away from the door and glanced around her apartment. Had it only been a few months ago when Nick swept into her life, baiting her into taking chances and having fun? She'd taken the biggest challenge of all, falling in love with Nick knowing that he might not return her love.

So much for getting back into the dating world again. She wished she'd never listened to Kate, never met Nick.

No, that wasn't true. What she really wished was that he could have loved her enough to get over his own fears. Maybe she was destined to be alone. A lonely women who made baskets for friends and family.

Without a clear goal, she went to the bedroom and started to empty her suitcase. On top of the clothing, in a silver frame that Nick's mother had given her before they left, was a snapshot of Nick. He smiled for the camera, his eyes carefree, his smile wide. He was devastatingly handsome. And he was gone.

She hugged it to her as her chest began to tighten. The tears didn't form until she placed the picture on her dresser and glimpsed the souvenir shell Nick had given her on their first date.

She picked it up and stroked it gently before replacing it. Suddenly lightheaded, she lowered herself to the bed, nearly sitting on the suitcase. She looked down and saw one of Nick's shirts. How had it gotten there? She didn't care. She grabbed it and held it to her face, inhaling the essence of Nick as tears streamed down her face.

Hot, burning drops rolled down her cheeks. She trembled and her breath came in jerky spurts. Curling up into a tight ball in the center of the bed, she rocked with pain. She wept for Nick and his inability to commit to a relationship. She cried for his parents, for the time and love they'd wasted, and how it hurt their son. But mostly, she mourned for a love lost, because she would never love anyone but Nick. He was forever a part of her, just as the sea would always reach the shore and the sky would be filled with stars. She knew that just as sure as Nick knew he had to leave.

After a while, the tears subsided. Jenny rolled on to her back and stared at the ceiling. Her body ached from the intensity of the tempest she'd just endured. Distracted, she watched the ceiling fan turn round and round, blinking when her vision became fuzzy.

A stray tear trickled down her cheek. She brusquely wiped it away. There may not be a chance to change Nick's mind about leaving, but she wasn't about to pine away. This would be the only time she gave in to her sorrow, she vowed. After today, she'd get her life back. Taking one last inhale of his shirt, Jenny tossed it across the room. She'd been fine before she met Nick. She'd be fine again.

Liar! screamed her inner voice.

A dull ache throbbed in her temples. Rising unsteadily, she went to the bathroom for some aspirin. She leaned against the sink as a wave of dizziness passed over her.

She took the pills to the kitchen, poured water in a

glass, and sat at the table. After swallowing the bitter tablets, she took a pad of paper and pen and started to make notes.

What started as an exercise in taking her mind off Nick only managed to make her realize that all the good things in her recent life were because of him. He reminded her how to live. In truth, he taught her to love. Too bad she couldn't do the same for him.

Chapter Fifteen

"Y ou're holding up well under the circumstances," Kate remarked as she sat across from Jenny at the kitchen table.

Jenny sipped her coffee. "It's been a month and I haven't called Nick. His office called with info on the Chandler job. I almost turned it down, but couldn't do that to Mr. Nelson. Besides, if Nick doesn't want to work with me, let his firm lose the job."

"You go, girl." Kate applauded. "I'm beginning to rub off on you."

Jenny laughed. It had been a horrible time, but she'd survived. There were moments when it seemed like her life was crashing down around her, but she kept moving ahead. The first week, she'd hoped Nick would come to his senses and return to her. If the telephone rang, she tried to calm the erratic beating in her heart. Disappointment always swept over her when it wasn't Nick.

"You may not believe this, but it gets better with time," Kate said quietly.

"Words of wisdom from the party girl?" At the hurt expression on Kate's face, Jenny became contrite, ashamed at criticizing her friend's heartfelt advice. "I'm sorry, that was uncalled for. Listen, I know you, Kate. I know you put on a show for everyone, always searching for the right guy, when your heart will always belong to one man. I know exactly how that feels."

Kate sat silently, pushing her cup in circles before her.

"You miss Alex, don't you?" Jenny asked gently.

She knew she hit her mark when Kate colored slightly. Waving her hand, she brushed away the question. "Hey, we're talking about you and Nick here. I just wanted you to know that I do understand. Breaking up is never easy." Kate looked into her drink. "Have you thought about dating anyone else?"

A fresh wave of pain hit Jenny. "No."

"Maybe there's still a chance," Kate encouraged.

Her forehead creasing into a frown, Jenny rose, crossing the room to pour herself another cup of coffee. "I really don't think so," she said, her heart sinking as she said the words.

"You told me that more than anything, Nick needs a solid relationship. Because of his family, he's convinced it'll never happen. Then he meets you, someone who believes in family and the sanctity of marriage. Of course he'd be attracted to you, you represent things he thinks are out of his reach." Kate toyed with the cup handle. "Then again, you two hadn't been dating for very long. How did you expect it to last?"

Jenny shrugged. "I guess I believed in us. At first I was concerned when he didn't say he loved me. But now that I look back, there were so many times he told me without saying the words. That kept me going, thinking things would work out for the best." She frowned. "Boy, was I wrong."

Kate raised an eyebrow. "You're sure about that?"

"I know Nick. He's defeated. And he won't risk hurting me again, not with the way he's been hurt."

"You know," Kate teased, "it's not very modern of you to sit around and wait for your man."

"Yes, well, I'm an old-fashioned girl and Nick is just as traditional in his views. I believe in true love. I thought he did, too."

"Believing is great, but for your sake, I hope you get over him soon."

Jenny grinned. "You are so single."

Another day passed and with it, Jenny's hopes. She stood staring out her office window, coming to the conclusion that she should allow for the possibility that he might be gone forever. She could only fool herself for so long. She had to start mending her broken heart.

Shaking her head, Jenny gazed at the busy street outside her window. She focused in on cars moving in and out of traffic, a pretty mindless exercise in forgetting about Nick. She did a double take when she saw a black Corvette pull into the stream of traffic from around the corner.

The hairs stood up on the back of her neck. Was it Nick's car? She craned her neck to get a better look, but the car moved too far away for her to tell.

Jenny walked to the desk and sank into her chair. Her heart beat so hard that she had trouble breathing. Was she seeing things? Did she want to see him so badly that her mind would play tricks on her?

Reality hit her hard when she thought about it. It means that a black car drove down the street and you're hopeful that it was Nick.

The door opened and a messenger carried in a beautiful arrangement of pastel pink carnations and lots of lacy baby's breath. He set them on the desk, grinning at her while she searched for a card. There was none, but in her heart she knew they were from Nick. He might have sent them anonymously, but she knew better.

An hour later, her phone rang. Hoping it was Nick, she hesitated a moment, taking a deep breath to steady herself.

"Hello, Jenny."

"Nick, what a pleasant surprise." She kept her voice calm and aloof, despite the fact that her knees were shaking. From the other end of the line silence screamed at her, then Nick cleared his throat.

"I was wondering if we could get together today."

"You mean like a date?"

"Yes. You could call it that."

"Actually, I'm busy. You could meet me Saturday, if you're really interested."

Disappointment filled his voice. "And where would that be?"

"At your house."

Jenny arrived at the lot shortly before noon. The mess had not been cleared. Obviously Nick hadn't been here since they returned from his parents.

She tried to stop the jitters and found that sitting in the confines of the car only made it worse. Leaving the vehicle, she walked through the remains of the structure, making mental notes as to what could be collected or thrown away. To her, it looked like most everything had to go. When Nick arrived, he'd know what they could salvage and what went in the trash heap.

Time ticked by and still Nick hadn't shown up. Jenny began to collect shingles, throwing them in one pile. Within a matter of minutes, her jeans were filthy, her hands muddy, and a streak of dirt ran across her cheek. Wisps of hair escaped from the ponytail as she bent over. To her chagrin, Nick picked that moment to drive up.

She waved in welcome, but he sat in the car, watching her from a distance. Intent on getting the job done, she shrugged and continued her work. As she leaned over to move a piece of lumber, she heard his car door slam.

"You should have gloves on," Nick admonished as he stormed up to her.

"I've never done this before. I was waiting for the expert to give me directions, but he's late."

"Wait, I've got some in the trunk." He jogged to the car, returning with two pairs. "Watch for nails. All I need is to take you to the emergency room."

"You're concerned about me?" she asked, innocent and wide eyed.

"Yes," he answered gruffly.

They worked in silence for an hour before Nick stopped. "This is crazy," he yelled at her. "Our relationship has crashed and burned and we're cleaning up a broken house!"

"A broken house?" She squelched the desire to chuckle at his absurd outburst when she glimpsed his somber expression. "Do you mean we still have a chance?"

"Come here. Let's sit down and talk." Nick took her hand, leading her to a safe place to sit.

"I've been miserable," he finally admitted. "And I've missed you."

Jenny tenderly touched his cheek, leaving a muddy smear. She tried to rub it off, but made a bigger mess. "Why didn't you call?"

He sighed heavily. "To be honest, I felt like a jerk."

He laughed and she imagined it was because of her stunned expression. "I guess that's not what you expected to hear."

"No."

He grinned sheepishly. "That's how I feel. I've been unreasonable, mule-headed, and a few other adjectives I won't repeat. I've made you unhappy and it was all so unnecessary." He looked past her for a moment, then brought his gaze to hers. "I've been trying to convince myself that I've been thinking logically, when all the time I knew in my heart I wanted you. Needless to say, I've made some decisions and I hope you'll agree with me."

"Let's hear them."

"First of all, I want to apologize for the way I've acted. You want me, not for my family connections or what I have. You've been honest with me all along and I know your feelings are genuine."

"Nick, I don't just want you."

His brows drew together in confusion. "What do you mean?"

"I love you."

His face softened. "You see, that's what I mean. I can see the truth in your eyes. If you were lying, I'd know it."

"Well I'm certainly not lying," she said with a huff. "And I do accept your apology."

Nick chuckled and touched her chin with his knuckles. "Thanks." He smiled and reached down to catch her hands in his. "Second, I want to explain why I've stayed away so long."

"This better be good."

"This is so tough. I don't know were to start."

"At the beginning?" she suggested.

"After I left you, I knew immediately that I'd made a major mistake. You weren't to blame for my problems, but I took it out on you anyway." He stared into her eyes and she saw the intensity burning there. "My pride kept me from returning. Then, after a few days, I had time to think about what I'd done and why. The more I dwelled on it, the answers that always seemed so out of reach started to become clear."

Nick smiled, inching closer as he spoke. "As a young boy I always looked up to my parents. Being a child, I never realized they had problems. When I finally noticed, it hit me hard. How could two people who I thought were in love hurt each other so much?

"Then my college sweetheart dumped me. I guess that's when I started to harden my heart and decided not to get seriously involved with a woman. Until you came into my life.

"From the start I was drawn to you, to your honesty. Those things had been missing from my life for a long time. You went fishing with me, taught me to waltz, even went along with the dating lessons. I found that I really liked you and I needed a friend."

"Everyone needs a friend."

He nodded. "But the old hurt returned and I kept

waiting for the bottom to fall out. That's why I shut you out. I couldn't deal with the emotions strangling me."

Jenny traced her finger over the back of Nick's hand. Burning memories raced through her mind. Memories of their first meeting, the lessons that were really excuses to date, and the day he walked out.

"When we went to my parent's house, I felt like I was drowning. I don't like what happened to my parents, but if they can forgive each other, how could I not?"

"That's a pretty good conclusion. It took you long enough."

"Yeah, the more I thought about it, the worse I felt for giving my mother grief all these years. I even called her to apologize."

"You did? Oh, Nick, I'm so proud of you. Louisa must be thrilled."

"She is and begged us to come back for another visit soon. I told her we had things to take care of first. I explained how your belief in us helped me to change and now I'm telling you how much I appreciate your faith in me."

She hugged him close, thankful that he'd come to these conclusions on his own.

Nick stood, reaching out his hand to help her up. "By the way, since we're talking about the house, I thought that maybe we could design a new one, together. We pretty much have to start from scratch, but I want you involved this time."

"Why?"

"Because I think we make a great team."

She considered that for a few moments, then wrapped her arms around his waist and hugged him close. "The original plans were fine with me, but I'd appreciate it if you would consult me on all decisions."

"I take it you don't mean just the house."

"You got it."

"Deal."

Resting her head on Nick's shoulder, with his arm firmly around her, Jenny sighed with contentment. Maybe the teacher had finally learned a few things from his pupil.

There was one issue Nick had evaded. She silently prayed he wouldn't let the moment pass without mentioning the only thing she wanted to hear.

He brushed her hair with his lips. "When I spoke to my mother, she made a point of saying that you're very special and that I was lucky to find someone who would put up with me."

Jenny laughed. "She's right you know."

"I know that." He stepped back and looked at her with somber eyes. "I really gave you a hard time. I don't deserve you."

"Yes you do."

He smiled. "Thanks. I owe you so much."

"You don't owe me a thing. I told you, I love you. I'd do anything for you."

Nick grinned, then a serious expression washed over

his face. "By the way. I've neglected to tell you something very important."

Her heart raced. "What's that?"

Nick tucked her tightly in his embrace. "I love you, Jenny. For now and for always."